DIAGNOSIS: LOVE

A Tennessee: Love Romance

Other books by Donna Wright:

Inadmissible: Love
Found: Love

DIAGNOSIS: LOVE

A Tennessee: Love Romance

•

Donna Wright

AVALON BOOKS
NEW YORK

Published by Thomas Bouregy & Co., Inc.
160 Madison Avenue, New York, NY 10016

Library of Congress Cataloging-in-Publication Data

Wright, Donna.
  Diagnosis: love / Donna Wright.
    p. cm.—(A Tennessee love romance)
  ISBN 0-8034-9745-8 (hardcover : acid-free paper) 1. Tennessee—
Fiction. I. Title. II. Series, Wright, Donna. Tennessee love romance.

PS3623.R5344D53 2005
813'.6—dc22

                    2005009739

PRINTED IN THE UNITED STATES OF AMERICA
ON ACID-FREE PAPER
BY HADDON CRAFTSMEN, BLOOMSBURG, PENNSYLVANIA

For the many people that support me as
I continue this crazy ride . . .

Chapter One

"You rang?" Alex Price strode purposefully into the urgent care clinic where he practiced medicine. Dressed in his jeans and a navy t-shirt covered by a pilot jacket, he didn't bother to even wear his name badge.

His receptionist held a finger to her lips to shush him then motioned for him to join her in the medicine room. Once they were safely inside with the door closed, she turned to him, her voice low and urgent. "Mr. Luft was here with a couple of men and a woman. I don't know what it's all about, but there was no stone left unturned. They went through all the offices, the patient rooms, files, everything."

"No hint as to what they wanted? You didn't hear anything?"

1

Marlene shook her head. "But I know how Luft feels about us, so I thought you should know. That's why I paged you."

By "us" she meant the clinic. Alex stayed in constant battle with Gordon Luft, the chairman of the board of the hospital that owned the clinic. Whatever his reasons for bringing people through the facility, they probably wouldn't be ones Alex liked.

"You were right to call me." He patted her on the shoulder and smiled.

As he opened the door to leave, his pager vibrated. Rather than the usual numeric memo, he had a text message: DANNI IN LABOR, MEET AT HOSPITAL.

He ran across the street to the hospital, ignoring questioning looks from his staff there. His younger sister, Tessa, waited for him on the steps of the hospital. Ready to dash to the obstetrics wing, he asked, "Is she okay?"

"She's fine." Tessa hugged him and took his hand. Without another word, however, he found he now held a leash.

From behind a large flowerpot trotted a miniature pot-bellied pig. In all the excitement, he hadn't noticed the lead.

"No you don't, Miss Tess. There's no way I'm pig sitting Joey while Danni has my first nephew."

She threw her blond hair back over her shoulder. "As our sister the ambulance chaser would say, possession is nine-tenths of the law," she backed away with a grin.

"I think not, baby sister."

"Who has the leash?" She walked up the few steps to the entrance. "Bye, bye!" The little wave and mischievous grin of victory stuck in his craw as she opened the door and entered the lobby.

Here I am, a full-fledged board certified physician, with a pig. Alex looked down at Joey who met his gaze with a grunt.

"I know!" Alex, with Joey hot on his heels, trekked up the stairs. "I'll take you to the pediatric wing and leave you with Darlene Thompson. Maybe she can use you in her pet therapy."

A pretty woman strode through the lobby doors toward him. Briefcase in hand, she walked by Alex with a courteous smile and curious look at the pig. As much of a hurry as he was in, he took a second look, and she was worth it. Long auburn curls, a sweet softly curved mouth, and heart-shaped face. Speaking of shapes, she wasn't exactly tall, but she held herself in a slim, willowy way, which didn't take away from the shapeliness of her figure.

Alex held the retractable leash securely, but neglected to lock Joey on the short leash. Before he knew it, the pot-bellied pig had advanced on the woman, sniffing and snuffling at her heels. In an effort to dodge him, she succeeded only in wrapping herself in the leash and tripping. Alex lurched forward in an effort to stop her fall and ended up with an armful of curvy female.

"Oh!" The woman crashed to the concrete steps, caught only by her hands, knees, and him.

Joey plopped down beside them with a snort and what looked suspiciously like a grin on his piggy face. Alex apologized profusely to her and tried to help her up. "I'm so sorry. He's never done anything like this before." Not exactly a lie. Sure, Joey had done some things like this before, but usually with Tessa and Danni. But then again, the pig and Alex had visiting relations at best.

He caught her under her shoulders and pulled her up until they were face to face.

Alex caught the flash of lace before she pulled herself together and pushed her full skirt back over her knees.

She stood with his help. "You have a pig." It was more a statement of fact than an accusation.

He couldn't imagine what this poor woman must be thinking. "As a matter of fact, yes, I do."

"Why?" She pulled her long auburn hair from her face. The eyes that met his were jade green. He couldn't tell if she were angry or just shocked. He figured probably a little of both.

He reminded himself of why he was even at the hospital on his day off. With a twinge of guilt for flirting with a beautiful woman while his sister was in labor, he still had to deal with this situation.

"Again I'm really sorry. Please let me examine you."

She took a step back. "Excuse me?"

The leash had let go of her, but Joey moved with her step. She looked warily down at the little guy as Alex continued, "I'm a doctor on staff here. I want to make sure you're all right." He pulled his ID badge from his pocket.

A rosy shade of pink started at her neck and blushed her entire face, including that perfect nose. She eyed Joey, who sat with a snort at her feet.

"I don't think so."

"Miss, according to hospital policy, you were hurt on this property and you have to be checked. I understand that my pig tripped you, but you still need to go through the risk management paperwork or I'm fired." *Which could very well happen anyway,* he thought wryly.

Joey had taken a seat next to the woman, staring at her with his big brown eyes. If Alex didn't know better, he'd swear the pig was in love.

Alex stooped to the pig's level, feeling his legs for breaks. "Joey, are you okay, boy?"

Joey pushed his snout against Alex, which he did instead of a hug, then licked the lady's knee. She didn't respond. He glanced at Alex then laid his hoof gently on her foot, as not to hurt her.

Alex chuckled. "I'm sorry. He obviously wants an introduction. This is Joey. He belongs to my sister."

She picked up his hoof and shook. "Hi, there, little guy. I'm Beth Chambers."

He licked her knuckles and Alex thought of a french courtier. He wondered if he could get away with kissing her hand? No doubt the answer would be a resounding no. *Oh, to be a pig.*

She bent over and rubbed him behind the ears, "He's so affectionate. I've heard about these pot-bellied pigs as pets, but never seen one in person."

Alex put his hands in his pockets and watched in fascination as the pig played with her. "I don't think he's ever shown this much affection to anyone."

"He's really cute." She stood straight and pulled her blazer tight.

He smiled, hoping she would trust him. "I'm Alex Price." He clipped his badge onto his coat. "If you'll just follow me into the lobby, you can see that all the nice volunteer ladies know me and I really am employed here."

Beth Chambers hadn't been this embarrassed since high school. That big leash had not only tripped her but during the fall she was sure this doctor, if that's what he really was, had seen every inch of her underwear. A shy woman at heart, Beth couldn't help but be humiliated. Of course, she had followed the old "you might have an accident" rule. But still, she was mortified.

She picked up her briefcase and followed the good doctor, if that's what he really was, to the front desk.

He didn't match her impression of doctors at all. He looked to be mid-thirties, which was a little young in her book. He didn't wear a white coat, nor did he have that air about him, that seriousness. He did have dark brown hair that she thought just missed being tamed, blue eyes that twinkled with a secret joke, and a lean runner's body. Other than those things, he wasn't anything special. Except his mouth, which always appeared to be on the verge of a smile.

Joey followed along, right behind Beth.

Dr. Price walked to the counter and put his hands on it. "Hey, Mona. That Christmas tree is great," he commented on a tabletop tree on the counter.

One would've thought the older woman just won the lottery with the way she lit up, but all she'd received was a lazy grin from this guy.

"Thank you, Dr. Price, I decorated it myself. Oh, I heard your sister is here. You must be so excited."

"You are so right. I am. But, you know Danielle has this pig from that court case she won a few years ago."

"Well, of course. I don't live in a cave, you know." Mona's snort sounded a lot like the pig's.

Beth smiled, *Note to self: find out pig story.*

"When she went into labor, she had the pig with her and now, unless I can find a way to get him up to the pediatrics wing, I can't go be with her. On top of that, this nice lady," he pointed at Beth, "needs me in the ER because she just fell."

"Oh, Dr. Price, I'll be glad to take Joey up to Dr. Thompson."

"Mona, I couldn't ask you to do that," he flashed a white grin at the older woman.

Oh, brother, Beth mentally groaned.

"You didn't." Mona waved away from his feeble protest. "I volunteered."

He nodded as he spoke and his mouth quirked with humor. "Ah, Mona. That's why you get the pink jacket, isn't it?"

She took Joey's leash. He brushed up against Beth's legs, licked her knee, and snorted at her, then followed the other woman obediently down the hall and to the elevators. "There, there. I'll take you upstairs. I'll bet the kids will love you there," Mona consoled him.

"Thanks, Mona." Alex called after the pair.

Beth pecked on his shoulder. He faced her.

"Is there a reason you can take a pig into this hospital? It appears to me that a pig, regardless of the cute factor, doesn't belong here."

"Pet therapy. It's on the pediatrics wing." He motioned with his head for Beth to follow him from the lobby down a hall.

"You put on quite the performance."

The doctor's sidelong glace held mild disdain. "So *you* say."

"It's not what I say, it's what I see."

He stopped walking and turned toward her, an

edge to his voice. "You don't know me. I'd appreciate it if you wouldn't make snap judgments."

"Fine, I won't." *At least I won't voice them.*

The few moments it took to reach the emergency room confirmed Beth's suspicions. Dr. Price spoke to everyone in the hall from fellow physician to the janitor. They all knew him. They all appeared to like him. Many stopped him on the way to tell a joke or just chat a moment.

Beth said nothing.

Dr. Price was a real piece of work, an actor, or better, court jester, with a license to practice medicine on the side. With the purposeful way he didn't fail to acknowledge anyone, he probably got away with everything.

She knew the type all too well. This kind of man used his powers for evil every time. She gave up her last position for just this very reason. *What kind of place is Gordon Luft running here, anyway?*

Once inside the ER, Beth followed Dr. Price to the desk, where he helped her check in. She noted his lack of "pig leash" in the version of the story he told the clerk. Of course, would he want anyone to know that he had the pig with him, or that he was the reason she fell?

Beth thought not.

He leaned over the counter, talking softly to the woman behind it. Whatever he said to her, the younger woman found it amusing with a little too much laughter. *Is every woman in this building fascinated with this guy, or what?* Beth thought, irritated with his oozing charm.

He picked up the receptionist's clipboard and appeared to review it. With a flirtatious grin he thanked the woman, who looked wistful when he turned from her.

"Miss Chambers—"

"*Ms*. Chambers, if you don't mind."

"Okay, *Ms*. Chambers. I've seen to it that Dr. Bailey sees you right away. Unless you want me to check you." Suddenly, he became clinical. She had no doubt he'd be professional if he did examine her.

"You'd better get to your sister."

"Oh, that's right!" He pulled out his cell phone.

"You can't use that here." Beth's voice left no doubt she wasn't joking.

"Yeah, yeah." He flipped it open and dialed.

She took the phone out of his hand and snapped it closed. "I mean that. You're a doctor, you know better than to use a cell phone in the hospital."

He huffed, "Are you the phone police, or something?"

"No, but I'm smart enough to make you follow a few rules."

"You know what?" He grabbed his phone back from her, a suggestion of annoyance hovering in his eyes. "I'll leave you with Dr. Bailey. She'll take good care of you and I'll join my family on the obstetrics wing." He took a few steps, then turned back to her. "And for the record, I'd already checked to see if any patients were using equipment the phone would interfere with. Nice to meet you."

As he walked toward the waiting room exit, she heard someone call after him. "Dr. Price! Dr. Price!"

He turned, still serious from his encounter with Beth. "Yeah, Cody, what's up?"

A nurse ran toward him. "We have a car accident. The six-year-old girl is shook up, but I need to take the mom in the back. She'll be fine, but I hoped you'd see to the girl. You're so good—"

"Go, go! Just show me my victim." His entire countenance changed from solemn to charming.

Another nurse led a pretty little thing in a Christmas sweatshirt by the hand.

He sat down with the child beside him. Beth sat on the other side of the child, wondering if she'd ever get out of there. If she weren't an administrator herself, she'd just leave. Her hands and knees were skinned, but she was fine. Not following policy, however, was a pet peeve for her. If she expected others to do it, she had to as well.

Of course, now there was a child to attend to and things were a little different. She wanted to see this guy in action. Was he all talk or could he make the little girl comfortable and work his magic on someone so honest as a mere child?

"I'm Dr. Price, what's your name?"

"Bernadette."

"Great name! Who were you named after?"

"My dad. He's Bernie."

"Makes sense. Say hello to Beth."

"Hello," the child grasped a dirty teddy bear closer. "Is my mommy gonna be okay?"

"Of course." Alex drew her attention back to him. "I'm a doctor, I know these things."

Beth felt empathy for the scared little girl and stroked her hair. "What's your bear's name?"

"Tom."

"Not Teddy?" Beth questioned with a smile.

"I don't know anyone named Teddy. Tom is my friend at school. He doesn't let big kids pick on me."

"Tom is a good friend. A good name for your bear, too."

A conversation ensued that included toys, Santa, and candy, especially chocolate.

Bernadette leaned forward and held a lock of Beth's hair for a long moment. "Your hair is a pretty color."

"So is yours," Beth countered.

"Mommy has the same color hair as me."

Not used to little ones, Beth lost the thread of conversation.

"Is my daddy coming here?"

Beth grabbed the moment to do something constructive. "I'll check."

When she came back from the counter, Alex and Bernadette were laughing and whispering, their heads close together.

Beth interrupted the joke. "Your dad should be here any minute, honey. Your mom is doing great. She'll be able to go home with you this evening."

The little girl looked at Alex. "You can't be here when Daddy gets here."

"Why not?"

"My daddy doesn't really like doctors and you shouldn't be here when he comes."

"He doesn't like doctors? Why not?"

"My daddy says doctors should all go to jail."

"Excuse me?" The amiable doctor had been thrown for the proverbial loop.

Beth wouldn't have missed this!

"He says they're all crooks. Are you a crook?"

"I don't think so. If I am, no one ever told me. Let's see. I brush my teeth before bed. I never litter. Do you think I'm a crook?"

He's back on kilter, Beth thought admiringly. She defended him, but she didn't know why. "Crooks never do those things."

"He says you make a whole lot of money. Daddy says you go on vacations all over the world. Where have you been?"

"Well . . ." he looked past the girl to Beth. "I've seen London, and I've seen France . . ."

Beth shot out of her chair and marched to the

desk. She'd heard and seen enough for one day. And, apparently, so had Dr. Price. She signed a form stating she was leaving without seeing the doctor and the hospital would have no culpability in her fall or injuries. Although she hated to break the policy, she justified that she'd signed all the proper paperwork. She started to leave then realized her briefcase remained tucked beneath her seat, beside the little girl and too close to smart-aleck Price. She sighed and veered to the couple. Bernadette giggled at Dr. Price's remarks as Beth approached.

Dr. Price stood and touched her arm as she collected her briefcase. "Where are you going?"

"I have to get home. Don't worry, I signed all the paperwork and left out any mention of a pig."

"Maybe I'll see you again?"

She'd stop this before he asked for her number. "Not if I see you first. Tell Joey I enjoyed meeting *him.*"

She strode away, hoping her gait held confidence. *I'm so unimpressed.*

"Sounds like that doctor made an impression on you." Rhoda Richardson breathed deeply as she continued her Tai Chi kata. Her slow precise movements were meant for relaxation. Rhoda talked while she did the unhurried dance, so Beth wondered how in the world she got any respite from it.

"The only impression that man made was a bad

one." Beth plopped down on Rhoda's sofa and picked up a bottle of dark liquid from an array of suspiciously smelling liquids lined up on the table. "What's this?"

Rhoda quit her movements. "Oh, it's apple cider vinegar and honey. It's cough medicine."

"Cough medicine? Do you have a cough?"

"No. But only because I use the medicine." She grabbed her bottled water from the coffee table. "Tell me more about your interview."

"The chances of Mr. Luft calling me and telling me I have that job are the same chances I have of marrying the doctor with the pig." She glanced at a notebook with a list scribbled inside it. "What's that?"

"Oh, that's a list of all the items I can do away with if I buy vinegar instead. Did you know you can eliminate ninety percent of the chemicals you use to clean and a third of your medicines just by using vinegar? But I can do this later; I want to hear about the doctor. I thought you said he looked good."

"Handsome in a way, yes. But he's a lot like, well, you know."

"Ah. Okay, he's handsome and friendly and manipulates people. You got all this from one quick meeting?"

"Don't give me the third degree. I'm not getting involved with someone else at work. Look how the last time ended."

"The guy who broke your heart did just that."

"I was played for a fool. I left a loser."

"You left the job because that was your choice. No one asked you to go. Anyway, if you're not going to get this job, then why worry about that aspect of the situation?"

"You don't understand. His sense of humor leaves me . . ."

"Amused?"

Beth arched a brow in warning.

"Sorry, but there's something in the way you've acted this evening that tells me you're interested. I feel these things, you know." Rhoda sat down next to Beth on the couch with her drink. The older woman put her feet on the coffee table.

"We've been neighbors for five years and every time you think I've found Mr. Right, he turns out to be crazy—"

"No," Rhoda argued. "Now that one had problems, yes, but he just needed a little TLC."

"Yeah, right. How about Jake, the one on the rebound?"

"It all worked out. He went back to his girlfriend and you had a great time with him while it lasted."

"Where did you get that four-one-one? We sat in *my* car eating hamburgers; in front of *her* house while he went on and on about how much he loved her. So far you're oh and two on the great date scale."

"Oh, that's right."

"Or—" Beth held a finger up to give her comments emphasis.

Rhoda took a drink of her water. "Don't say it, Beth. Just leave it alone."

"He turned out to be wanted by the police."

"I said leave it alone, didn't I?" Rhoda huffed.

"You fixed me up with a guy wanted in Atlanta. How lucky can I get?"

"Just for questioning, that's all. He never did get indicted. It was *just* to ask a few questions."

"Either way, your *feelings* always get me into trouble. I'm not interested in this guy and his pig, anyway."

"If you say so." Rhoda poured a drink into a glass from a plastic pitcher sitting on the table. "Try some vinegar and grape juice. It's good for your weight. Gives you—" she broke off to sip at the liquid, and made a face that said the concoction left a bad taste in her mouth. "Energy. Whew!"

"Whenever I see someone eat or drink something and make that face, I just say no."

"Even though we spend every holiday together and have for five years, and we're best friends who tell each other every thought and feeling, you still don't trust me."

"Not with my love life. You're right."

Rhoda tossed a throw pillow at her. Beth responded by throwing it back.

Before it turned into a free for all, Beth's cell phone rang and she pulled it from her purse then flipped it open. "Beth Chambers."

"Miss Chambers, Gordon Luft here. I'd like to know if it's true you fell on the hospital steps on the way out this afternoon?"

"I wasn't injured in any way. Is there a problem?"

The man heaved a disgusted sigh. "No, of course not. I suppose then we'll meet in my office tomorrow. Can you be here around nine in the morning?"

"Of course. I'll be glad to hear your decision."

"Well, goodbye then." He rang off without another word.

Rhoda eyed Beth. "What was that all about?"

"I'm not sure, but I think I got the job." She sat back and grinned.

Alex went straight home after Danni brought his nephew into the world. He looked at the bedside clock. Fifteen hours of labor, but she was a real trooper. *I knew it would be a boy all along.* Ecstatic Danni and the baby did so well, but Alex was tired and due back at work in just a few hours.

When his home phone sounded, he almost jumped from his skin. He only had a few hours to rest; hopefully it wasn't a hospital emergency.

"Price."

"Alex, it's Darlene Thompson. I came into work this morning to a pig in one of my pet therapy cages and I have a note saying he's yours. What's this all about?"

He sat down on the bed in self-disgust. He'd forgotten the pig. "Joey belongs to my sister."

"Sorry, pal, I'm not a kennel service. Luft will have my head on a platter and news is the new administrator starts today."

That *was* news. "I'll be right there to get him."

On the way back to work, Alex thought only of sleep. How nice it would be to get into the bed and just rest until his body said, "Alex, time to get up now." No pager. No alarm clock. No phone. Just his body, in a soft quiet voice, telling him gently, time to wake.

By the time he got Joey home to Danni's and both he and the pig fed, it would leave him little time to clean up and get to work. It would save time to head straight to the doctor's lounge and clean up there.

But, after a good hot shower, the mirror held no lies. His hair looked like it needed a good cut. He promised himself every day last week he'd have it done, but the time never presented itself. His eyes were red from lack of sleep, and putting his contacts in was torture. That left him wearing his glasses, a royal pain. He shoved the wire frames up on his nose as he strode through the hospital at a steady pace, ready to meet the afternoon and evening planned for him at the clinic.

"There's Dr. Price. He runs the urgent care clinic." Alex stopped and turned around to see Gordon Luft and alongside him, spiffy in a three-piece suit that couldn't hide her trim figure, Ms. Chambers from yesterday's mishap.

"Nice to see you again, Ms. Chambers." *Don't let her be here about the accident,*

"Have you two met?" Alex caught the questioning look Mr. Luft gave.

"When I fell yesterday, Dr. Price . . . helped me."

"Hmph. Well," Luft took his glasses off his face and cleaned them as he spoke, "I didn't realize the good doctor was with you when you checked in at the ER."

Alex sighed. Why did he feel like a kid in middle school when he was around Luft? "I saw her fall. It was appropriate for me to walk her back there."

"Uh huh."

Ms. Chambers cleared her throat. "I was treated just fine, Mr. Luft. Dr. Price was the perfect gentleman."

"I didn't hire him to be a perfect gentleman, I hired him to be a physician. One I can trust patients with. One who shows up for work on time."

"Actually, Gordon, I'm an hour early. I don't go on until noon today."

Ms. Chambers spoke before he had the chance to get away. "How's your sister?"

"She and my new nephew are fine. Thanks for asking."

Luft just couldn't leave it alone. "Isn't that the sister who has the famous pig?" He turned to her. "It's quite a story, really. His sister is an attorney and her—well, now he's her husband—also an attorney, were in this huge custody battle. Neither one bothered to find out it was a pig and not a little boy."

She appeared amazed. "Really? What happened?"

Alex completed the story, his way. "When their clients, who both wanted the pig for ulterior motives, decided they'd done all the damage they could with the little guy, they abandoned him. Michael, Danni's husband, ended up with him, but then they got married. So, Danni has a dog, a pig, and now a son. Cole Alexander Sommers."

"They named their son for you. You must be honored." Beth Chambers appeared authentically touched.

"Yeah. I'm excited. So, if you two will excuse me—"

"Dr. Price, I think you should know Ms. Chambers is the new administrator." His bating tone grated Alex.

He looked over his glasses at his nemesis. "Excuse me?"

Luft had to enjoy this. "I'm saying she's now your supervisor. Isn't it nice?"

He couldn't hold back the grin. "Are you saying you bypassed the board and hired Ms. Chambers?"

Luft defended his actions. "I acted with board authority."

He couldn't go into any more detail with Ms. Chambers standing there. He didn't want to scare her off on her first day, but all he could think of was the reactions of a few of the other doctors, and board members for that matter, who abhorred women in positions of power.

Daggers lit Luft's eyes. If looks could kill, Alex would be dead.

"Personally, I think it's great. Welcome aboard, Ms. Chambers. I wish you the best."

This time, he walked away without turning back.

Beth followed Mr. Luft to her new office. "What was Dr. Price trying to say out there?"

"Dr. Price is a problem we'll discuss at a different time." He stopped, unlocked the door, then handed her the key.

"This is your office."

He opened the door and she entered first. The room, cold from lack of use, needed more than a fire in a non-existent fireplace. It needed someone in there to make things happen.

Beth smiled at the challenge.

"I'm sure this will be fine." A large cherry desk sat in front of a window, facing her. The huge overstuffed leather chair behind it welcomed her. She wanted to dance on the desk in excitement, but chose to lay her briefcase on it instead. "This will be fine," she repeated the words for lack of anything else to say.

After two months of being unemployed, never expecting to find a job before the first of the year, and now this. A hospital administrator, her dream job, her luck amazed her.

"You can put pictures of family on your desk, of course. We don't have any policy forbidding that."

Beth didn't give anything away. "I'll keep that in mind."

Luft continued, "I'll start interviewing girls for a secretary position tomorrow."

"I'd rather do my own hiring, thank you."

Luft scrutinized her over his glasses. "I normally do all the hiring."

She stood her ground. "I like to know what I'm getting."

A long moment passed before he spoke again. "I see. Then, if you'll excuse me."

She closed the door behind him.

"Mine, mine, all mine." She walked around the office, taking note of every minute detail. After she sat down in the large, very comfortable chair, she called human resources and asked for a list of candidates for her new assistant.

Assured she would receive them immediately, she opened her briefcase, took out her dictaphone and some information Mr. Luft gave her. After an

hour of dictating memo after memo and a few let-
ters, she took a moment to relax.

A knock on the door pulled her from her reverie.
A silver-haired woman entered. "Hello, Beth. I'm
Lucy. I'll be your interim assistant. Let me know if
there's anything you need."

"How nice of Mr. Luft to send you."

"Who, dear?"

"Mr. Luft."

Confusion wrote itself on the woman's face.
"I'm sorry?"

"The chairman of the board."

"Oh. Of course, he's very nice."

Beth could see it written on her face, the woman
had no idea who Beth was talking about.

"How did you come to be here?"

"That cute little blond girl in personnel sent me."

Regardless of how the woman got there, Beth
needed an assistant and waved her to a chair. "Please,
Lucy, take a seat. We'll need to get acquainted."

"Thank you." She sat down across from Beth.

"First, I like to keep things professional. So, if
you don't mind, I prefer to be called Ms. Chambers
to anyone who calls."

"All right."

"I need some confidential information tran-
scribed as soon as possible. Can you do that?"

The older woman leaned forward. "Do what?"

"Transcribe. Can you transcribe?" *Uh oh. Maybe not so good, after all*, Beth thought.

"Oh, no. Only a doctor can transcribe." Lucy shook her head.

Confusion caught Beth by surprise. "No, I think you mean prescribe, and you're right. Only a doctor can prescribe medications. What I referred to was, can you listen to a tape of me speaking and type it out?"

"Oh, that!" The woman laughed. "No, the words get jumbled and my fingers cramp up awful. But I make a great cup of coffee and answer the phone really well." She picked up the handset of Beth's phone. "Do you want to watch?"

Chapter Two

Alex strode to his car, wanting to climb in and sleep in the backseat. He hadn't been this tired since he interned, and dreaded the thirty-minute trip home. Of course, the day had been worth every second of lost rest.

He thought a moment about the woman he'd sent to the hospital for a breast ultrasound. He opened his cell phone and dialed radiology. "Hey, Gus, Alex Price. How you doing?"

"All's well up here, Alex. Hey, I got your patient with the breast lump up here. Ultrasound showed it's a cyst."

"That's great. I wondered about her."

"I knew that's why you called. Your patient was sent to her gynecologist to drain that."

27

"Thanks, Gus. You're the best." He closed the phone with a smile.

Now, he could concentrate on his new nephew, whom he stopped to see on his way to the car. He and Danni were to be released from the hospital tomorrow.

He pulled his car from the parking garage.

As he maneuvered into traffic, he opened his phone again. There was a guy out of work that he gave a sample of antibiotics to so he could be ready to look for a job. He knew a girl from college who owned some oil and lube shops. Alex thought he might at least get him an interview. She wasn't in but he left her a voicemail.

The truth was he and Marlene spent as much time putting patients together with resources as he practiced medicine.

God knew it was needed in the community.

He'd heard rumors, though, rumors of closing the clinic. He hated that people spread around these speculations. The clinic, by its nature, would never make money, that didn't bother him. The board, however, had always hated it. They only opened it in the hopes people would see the goodwill to the community and use Trentville Memorial instead of driving the extra thirty minutes to Ft. White.

According to the figures, the plan had some validity. Unfortunately, Luft and friends gave the credit elsewhere.

His cell phone rang. "Price."

"Dr. Price, it's Marlene."

His administrative assistant usually didn't call him so something was definitely up. "Everything okay?"

"Of course, I just checked out the money and made the deposit at the hospital."

"Hey, I only practice medicine, you're the money woman. What does all that mean?"

She snickered. "I balanced my cash drawer and took the money to the hospital so they can make the deposit. I've taught you all this before."

"I know. I'll never be a good receptionist or cashier. So you have to work for me forever."

"Those were my plans, exactly. Guess who I ran into at the hospital?"

"Santa Claus?"

"You *are* tired if that's the best you can do. No, Lucy Ledbetter."

"The little lady who worked for years doing odd clerical jobs for administration?"

"That's the one." Her voice filled with humor, he could tell she nearly giggled.

"Is she sick?"

"No. She's working."

"Working? She's retired."

"She's the interim assistant to the new administrator."

"You've got to be kidding! She's been retired

since before the Dead Sea was sick. Lucy Ledbetter can't answer the phone."

"Sure she can, just not necessarily with the right name. Ms. Chambers, which by the way is what everyone is supposed to call her, is not very happy, at least not from what I've heard from my sources."

Alex didn't want to know who Marlene's sources were. He just knew that they usually knew the truth, with a little seasoning, like salt. In fact, a grain of salt often didn't do it, more like a pound of it worked better.

"And don't forget, I won't be in tomorrow. We're closed because of the meetings you have tomorrow and Dr. Ellis is out of town and can't cover for you. Remember your meeting with Mr. Luft, too. He's not going to keep buying you're too busy to meet with him."

"I know. You have a good day off and don't worry about the clinic or me. Okay?"

"Will I have a job to come back to?" She didn't bother to hide the worry in her voice.

He wouldn't lie to her. "Hopefully."

Marlene rang off.

Alex hated the situation of not having control of the clinic's future. After all, they did good work. The hospital should be thanking the staff, but the bottom line was all anyone thought about.

Would Ms. Chambers make a difference? Did

she want to? He had a meeting tomorrow morning with the Chief of Staff and one tomorrow afternoon with Luft. Maybe he could maneuver his way into Ms. Chamber's office and good graces.

He rubbed his burning eyes. After getting some sleep he'd take a shot.

The next morning, Alex felt much better. He put in his contacts, which in itself added to the day. After a brisk shower and a hot cup of coffee, he pushed the button for the elevator that took him from his loft to the parking garage.

The drive wasn't so bad after a good night's rest and some caffeine. The radio blared the news and some soft rock and he hummed along as he drove his old Chevy Nova down the divided highway to Trentville.

Before any appointments, he went in to see Danni and Cole, who were readying to leave that day.

"You got everything?"

"Oh, hey, big brother." Danni kissed him on the cheek. "I have it all, I think. I'm glad I decided to come here to have him. Everyone knows you and I got all kinds of extras. Ice cream, soup, anything I wanted."

He helped her sit in the wheelchair. "They'd have done that anyway. They're really good here."

A nurse brought the baby into the room and laid him in Danni's arms.

"I'm waiting on Michael. He's getting the car, but he wanted to wheel me out for some reason."

"I can't speak for him, sis, but I'd say it's pride."

She cooed at the baby. "I suppose. But, don't the staff usually take care of that?"

"If my sister wants her husband to wheel her out, then he will."

He kneeled down in front of her to get a better look at Cole. I always knew babies were little, I've even delivered a few, but it's so different when it's yours."

"Yours?"

"I mean one I love."

"I know," she spoke softly. "You need to find someone, Alex. I know you love that clinic, but it can't keep you warm at night."

He avoided meeting her eyes.

"Here." She handed him the baby. "See what you're missing."

Alex walked the room with Cole, talking softly to the sleeping child. The warmth of the baby touched him to his soul. His little hands and nose were so perfect.

After only a few minutes, Michael entered. He spoke in hushed tones, "Are you ready, hon?"

"I am." Danni took the baby when Alex offered him to her.

Alex and Michael hugged and slapped each other on the back.

"How's Joey?" Danni asked over her shoulder as Michael wheeled her out.

"He's fine. The house is ready and waiting on you."

As Alex strode to his meeting, he smiled because he knew what a festive homecoming they would have. He and Tessa hired a maid service to clean the house thoroughly and place balloons and flowers everywhere.

Danni and Mike left for home with the baby and Alex continued his day.

After his medical staff meeting, he went in search of his new supervisor, Ms. Chambers. Outside her office, Lucy sat quietly reading a large print book her lips moving to the words. He waited a long moment, then cleared his throat.

She looked up as if she had no idea who he was. He was used to that look from Lucy. "May I help you?"

"Hi, Lucy. Remember me? I helped you that time you fell at your house and your daughter brought you to the emergency room."

"Well, of course, I remember. How could I forget?" He saw in her eyes she had no idea what he meant.

"Is Ms. Chambers here?"

Her voice altered to hushed tones. "Oh, yes. There's a woman in there with her. They aren't happy."

"How do you know that?"

"Oh, a good secretary knows these things."

Just then the door opened and Dr. Thompson exited Ms. Chamber's office. When the door closed behind her, Dr. Thompson looked at him. Lucy may have been right; she didn't look happy. "I wondered how long it would take before you came waltzing in here."

Alex didn't quite understand her remark. "Your point being?"

"You'd better get in there and make her like you, and all of us, for that matter. I'm afraid Luft will have her cut the pet therapy program."

He cursed inwardly. "Then I'm not far behind."

"Probably not. But, I may have a chance. She can't make any decisions until after the board meeting, next month."

"What will you do?"

"I'll be allowed to stay in pediatrics, but the therapy is probably history. No matter how much we impact the kids."

"Did she actually say that?"

"No, but I got the picture." She folded her arms over her chest.

For lack of words, Alex nodded.

"Go in there, Alex. You can win over the devil himself. I've seen you sell pigs ham sandwiches. Talk to her. Explain who we all are. Tell her how we all fit into this community and how much good this hospital does here."

Alex smiled, warily. "Okay. I'll see what I can do."

Darlene left him to it. He marched to the door without being announced, but Lucy was asleep so it didn't really matter. Before he knocked on the door, he watched the older lady for a long moment, then went and put his fingers on her neck just to make sure. Yep, there was a pulse.

He returned to the door, and knocked before he opened it. "Ms. Chambers?"

She sat at her desk with a laptop computer in front of her. "Dr. Price. Didn't you check with Lucy? I'm not open for an appointment right now."

This is going to be a challenge, Alex thought with a smile, "Your assistant sleeps softly, even as we speak."

Not even a grin. "Well, since you're here, you may as well sit down."

For the sake of the clinic, he followed orders. "I wanted to get to know you since we're going to be working together—"

"Dr. Price, you don't need to get to know me. We're not going to be friends. I'm not here to make friends; I'm here to do a job. Is there anything else?"

Alex's face grew hot. "I'm just trying to be nice."

She leaned forward, green eyes gleaming.

"You're trying to find out whether or not I'm closing your clinic."

"Are you?"

She pushed her chair back from the desk and smiled. Unprepared for the effect that smile had on him; he took a deep breath.

"Actually," she said in a much gentler tone, "I am concerned. The clinic is quite a drain on hospital resources."

"So, you'll close it because of that?"

"I don't have that authority, it goes to the board."

"Then, Luft will have you close me, and he'll come out smelling like a rose in the community while you'll take the heat."

She looked thoughtful. "I have no idea what I'm going to do, so I don't want to lie. But, I will tell you this much. The clinic is not the first thing on my list of things to do. Like every other part of the hospital, it will be evaluated."

He stood. "I appreciate your honesty."

She walked around her desk, leaning back on it, arms crossed, her expression intent and serious. "Another thing, Dr. Price. I meant what I said about friends at work. That becomes too complicated."

"Does that come from experience, Ms. Chambers?"

She ignored him. "That doesn't mean I'll be unfair to anyone, or that I'm the type of person to single out people, or departments, for persecution."

"Fair enough."

Beth's intercom sounded. "Ms. Williams, there's a Mr. Steinberg here to see you."

Beth closed her eyes and counted to three. "Send him in."

Beth knew it didn't matter who was out there, if the woman couldn't remember her name, how was she expected to recognize the person standing in front of her?

How embarrassing with Dr. Price's blue eyes intently on her.

Gordon Luft entered her office. "I think you'd better find a replacement for your assistant soon."

Dr. Price put his hands in his pockets. "Whose idea was Lucy's position here, anyway?"

The older man appeared startled. "I didn't see you there, Price. Lucy? Well, I'm not sure."

"Oh, I think you are, Gordon. I think you put her here for a reason."

What reason? Beth simmered. If she were being set up, she'd hang Luft.

He ignored the doctor's remark. "I need you to go to Lexington on a business trip next week, Ms. Chambers."

"I see. What's this for?"

"It's the Kentucky Hospital Association's annual conference. They're usually pretty good. I'd go, but with you here, I'll send you. The information will be invaluable."

"I just got here I'm surprised you'd want me to go somewhere so soon."

"I think it will be worth the hospital's money to send you, Ms. Chambers." He then turned to the good doctor. "Don't you have somewhere to be?"

"Only in your office. You wanted to see me this afternoon." Price couldn't make it any more obvious that he enjoyed quarreling with Luft.

"I've changed my mind. You can go home, or do whatever it is you do."

Beth didn't miss the intensity of Dr. Price's gaze on Mr. Luft. Though she knew him to be good-natured just from the meetings they'd had, there was something angry in his look.

"Thank you for seeing me, Ms. Chambers." With that, Dr. Price left.

Gordon Luft wasted no time. "Did you tell Dr. Thompson to get rid of that zoo?"

"I told her what I'm telling all the department heads who come to my office. I will evaluate each department and try to either fix it, save it, or just leave it alone. You're asking me to make recommendations without looking at all the facts."

Luft turned every shade of red. "Let me tell you something, young lady. I hired you because you're supposed to be cost-efficient."

"You hired me, Mr. Luft, because I fell on your front steps and you're afraid I'll sue you."

He opened his mouth to say something, but nothing came out. Finally, he asked, "How . . . did—"

"I know? I made some calls and put some numbers together. I heard you'd never hire a woman for this position. That you already had another candidate ready to give notice on *his* present job."

"You think you're smart, don't you?" Luft didn't hide his anger.

"Not as smart as I could be, but much smarter than you'd ever give me credit for. Now, if you'll excuse me, I'm going to look over the brochure for this conference. I've been to it the last two years. You're right. It's a good one."

Alex looked at the envelope for a third time. For the life of him he couldn't think of a soul that would have done a favor for him like this. Inside the envelope, folded in a sheet of blank, white paper lay a ticket to the Lexington conference Luft and Ms. Chambers had discussed. Not only that, a hotel reservation confirmation for the entire weekend. The brochure included workshop descriptions, some already circled in red. Those tracks focused on information regarding urgent care clinics, sliding scale collections, pay-at-time-of-service offices, and grants for nonprofit facilities.

He grew excited at those prospects.

"Hey, Marlene!"

His administrative assistant peered around the door. "Yes?"

"Who do we know that would sponsor me to a conference?"

"Maybe Luft in the hopes you wouldn't return, of course," she deadpanned.

"Of course," he smirked. "You should leave the Luft jokes to me. After all, I *am* the funny one."

As she strolled from his office she threw over her shoulder, "That's a matter of opinion."

He studied the brochure one more time. "Maybe this fell from Heaven. Maybe it's not even real."

As he saw patients, Marlene took the time to confirm, by phone, all the reservations. When the day was over, he went to the cashier's window. "So, am I on my way to Lexington?"

She appeared a little stunned as she answered, "Yeah, as a matter of fact you are, but they wouldn't give me any information at the conference headquarters or the hotel regarding who made the arrangements. They all acted as if you'd done it yourself."

He slipped into his pilot's jacket. "This is borderline eerie."

Marlene put her coat on. "Well, as far as I can see you're going to Kentucky. Oops. Forgot to turn off the Christmas tree lights." She opened the side door to the reception area.

As Marlene finished, the front door opened and

Alex heard another female voice. "I'm Ms. Chambers. Is Dr. Price still here?"

Alex opened the side door. "At your service. What's up?"

Marlene exited the clinic door, calling over her shoulder, "Goodnight, Dr. Price."

"Night, Marlene."

"I was on my way home and wanted to drop off some administrative forms for you. I would leave them with your assistant, but since you're here—"

"Or, you could have let *your* assistant bring them." Alex let his expression fill in the unspoken words. If Lucy brought the forms, he'd get them by the fourth of July, at best.

"You had to rub that in, didn't you?"

"Be careful, Ms. Chambers. You were almost friendly." He couldn't believe it. The friendly banter was the closest she'd come to a joke yet. Maybe he could wear her down after all.

The door opened again. Joey trotted through it followed by Alex's sister, Tessa.

Joey immediately went and sat down beside Ms. Chambers, then licked her knee.

Tessa appeared stunned. "I'm so sorry. I've never seen him do anything like *that*." She pulled on his lead, but Joey resisted.

Alex panicked. He didn't want Ms. Chambers to think he kept Joey with him in the office. It wasn't like she was his biggest fan, and to be honest, beautiful or not she was the boss. "Ms. Chambers, this is my sister, Tessa. Tessa, I'd like to introduce Ms. Chambers, she's the new hospital administrator."

Tessa's eyes became as big as saucers as she grasped the situation instantly. As Ms. Chambers rubbed Joey behind his ears she tried to help Alex as much as possible. "Please don't think I bring him here all the time. I'm just dropping by to ask Alex a few questions about the holidays. Joey needed to get out and my sister, she just had a baby . . ." her voice trailed.

Ms. Chambers stood upright. "The clinic *is* closed, and though I would normally frown on an animal in here, I know your situation."

Alex relaxed somewhat and watched the little guy rub himself all over her legs. "And he's got a crush on you, Ms. Chambers."

"He is the sweetest little guy." She took a step toward Alex to hand him the envelope she carried and Joey cut her off mid-step. The next thing anyone knew, Ms. Chambers lay in Alex's arms. Joey squealed and ran around their feet as Tessa tried to grab his leash.

As he set her right, Alex asked Beth, "You okay?" *And, do you always smell like a field of wildflowers, or is today special?*

"I'm fine. He has a habit of tripping me, doesn't

he?" She made a sad attempt at a laugh but her blush deepened.

By this time, Tessa had caught Joey's leash and untangled Alex and Ms. Chambers.

Alex smiled as he helped her stand straight. "I hope he didn't hurt you."

"No, really, I'm fine," she reacted. It was slight, but he saw it in her eyes. She liked him more than she wanted him to know.

And, for some reason, it made Alex smile.

Tessa piped in, "Please don't be angry with Alex, I just stopped in for a minute, knowing the clinic was closed. I didn't expect to see anyone here, nor did I think Joey would do any harm. I've just taken him out for my sister because she claims he's bored."

Ms. Chambers waved away their fears. "I'm fine, really."

Alex bent over and picked up the envelope she'd dropped in all the confusion. "Sorry. I'll get right on these."

She turned to Joey, who pulled at his leash to go to her. "As for you, Hamlet, come here."

Tessa dropped his leash and he went immediately to Ms. Chambers and put his head against her knee. "You're so cute I can't be mad at you."

Thank goodness, Alex smiled at her as she said her goodbyes to Tessa and left.

Alex grabbed Joey's leash so he couldn't follow her out of the building.

"Joey you deserve a big pouch of pig chow. You just broke the ice for me with my new supervisor. You cute, sweet thing," he echoed Ms. Chamber's words.

Tessa and Alex talked about holidays and family matters while Alex locked up.

"So, it's settled then." Tessa appeared happy with her plans. "We all meet at Mom's on Christmas Eve. You're spending the night. We'll meet you there Christmas morning and bring Brian's dad, too."

They walked toward their cars in the cold. Tessa asked him about his plans for the evening. "I don't have anywhere to go tonight."

"You want to come over and eat? I'm fixing lasagna for Brian. He'll share."

"No, I think I'll just go home and kick back."

"Alone?"

"That's the best way to relax."

"And why is that, Dr. Price? None of us ever hear you mention anyone. Why isn't there someone waiting on you, big brother?"

He didn't find her questions out of place. "Are you kidding? With my schedule? What woman would want that, Tess?"

They stopped at their cars, parked side by side. "I think that some ladies in the area are missing the boat."

He opened his door and started the car, then stood up again. "You need to remember who I am. A lot of people get into medicine and make a killing. I just want to make a living. Some of the women I've met lately see the word doctor and think I'm made of money."

"That doesn't mean there's not someone out there."

"Nope, and I hope there is. I see Mom and Dad, you and Brian, and Danni and Mike. You've all found these great loves. I won't settle for anything less."

"Maybe you won't have to." She let him open her car door.

"We'll see." He smiled at her. "Now, get in your car and get out of here, I want to go home."

"Goodnight, big brother."

He waved her off as she left.

When he got home, his answering machine blinked with a message from his mechanic. The exhaust system for his car had arrived and next week he needed to have it put on. But, he'd wait until after the conference. Usually when he had the old green girl worked on, it came with at least another five hundred dollars of discovered work he hadn't figured into the budget. Maybe his dad was right, maybe he needed to break down and buy another car. But, he'd had this one for almost twenty years. She'd been through high school, college, and med school; it seemed a shame to dump her when she needed him most.

He tried to watch a cop show on TV, but found himself nodding off. Tiredness got the best of him and he went to bed. He'd think about the car later.

The McKinley House, a beautiful hotel in the heart of Lexington, served as an outstanding backdrop for the conference. The flurry of activity around Beth as people networked, bought chances for non-profit organizations, looked at medical computer systems, and found their way to workshops motivated Beth to enter the game.

She chose a two-hour lecture on taking charge in a new position of management. It covered everything from the best information systems to finding the right staff. Maybe it would help her find a good assistant. That part alone had caught her eye on the handout.

She also needed a way to let Lucy down easy. The older lady was slowly boring a way into Beth's heart. However, she'd come in on Friday with two different shoes on the wrong feet. Beth shook her head. Luft sent her Lucy for a reason, she knew. Considered "as needed" for payroll purposes, the woman was loved by one and all. Beth didn't want to be the one who let the woman go, but she thought that might be part of his plan.

Once the session ended, she took her briefcase

and joined the group exiting the room. She wished she'd chosen more comfortable shoes as she pulled herself from the throng of people and found a quiet place along the wall to view the schedule again. Even though her heels weren't high, her feet still throbbed.

Before being offered the job at Memorial, Beth had planned to be here, more to job-hunt than to attend workshops. She was glad that she'd still had the chance to come. Even though she had only attended the one session, it had been worth her time. But then, she reminded herself, she'd always enjoyed the Kentucky conference.

Dina Kimball found her leaned against the wall. She wondered if Dina were in a position to move. She'd been in Nashville for at least six years. She might make a good addition to Trentville Memorial.

"Beth Chambers! You still at Laurence County?"

"Hello, Dina." Beth hugged her. "I'm at Trentville Memorial now. How about you?"

"Still at Nashville Medical. Probably retire from there."

"So, did Candi come with you?" Beth mentioned a colleague of Dina's.

"Candi got married and moved to Arkansas. The only person I've seen so far from last year is Frank Blair. That's why I thought you were probably still at Laurence County."

Glad for the warning, Beth told Dina about the

new job, leaving out the parts about the pig, and Frank being the reason she left L.C.

To attend other sessions before lunch, the ladies parted with promises of getting together some time during the weekend.

At lunch on Saturday, she caught a glimpse of Alex. He sat at a table with Dina. They laughed a lot, she noticed while she tried not to stare. *This is supposed to be business. Not fun time, Dr. Price. You don't need yet another female under your spell.*

A gentleman at her table showed interest, but Beth couldn't take her eyes off Dr. Price long enough to make any real conversation. The guy, who was actually kind of cute, finally gave up and began talking to others at the table.

Uncomfortable after blowing the guy off, she rose to leave. She saw Alex stand and motion her to their table. If she didn't go, Alex might think her sick and follow her. If she did she'd have to watch him charm another woman. Either way, she didn't like it. As she approached, he asked, "You're not leaving before the speaker begins, are you?" Concern laced his voice.

"I thought I'd take a few moments to go to my room and take a breather."

"Oh, Beth, sit!" Dina gestured towards the chair beside her. "We all already know each other and need to get better acquainted."

She sat in the chair on Alex's other side. Beth

knew Dina from past conferences well enough to know she'd set her sights on Alex. Dina lived in Nashville, which was almost four hours from Trentville. Beth didn't see it happening. She didn't know, however, if Dina was focused enough to make it work.

Alex motioned for a server. "Could you please bring us another glass of water and, Ms. Chambers can we get you anything?"

His sincere attitude ran guilt through her. "I'm fine, thank you. And, since we're not at the hospital, you can call me Beth."

"I don't want to make you uncomfortable, but I'll try . . . Beth." His soft tone left her breathless. How could the sound of her own name mean anything to her? She'd heard it all her life, but his voice made it, what was the word she looked for? Special? No, intimate. A feeling passed through her, one she hadn't had in a long time, if ever. Alex Price, with all his charm, had depth as well. She saw it when he talked to little Bernadette in the ER. She noticed how people always respected him in the hospital. Truth was, he cared about people and they responded to that.

A dangerous combination when balanced with his humor and charisma.

Dina's gaze fell heavy on Alex for a long moment. Then she looked at Beth with a false sparkle in her voice. "It's really good seeing you, but if you need to

go to your room, we'll understand. Won't we, Alex?"
She touched his sleeve.

Before he could answer, Beth scrutinized Dina.
"I'm okay. I think I'll just sit here and listen to the
speaker."

Alex smiled. "Why go upstairs when you have a
free lunch and friends to sit with?"

"Right. I appreciate you sharing your table
with me."

"No problem." Alex offered Beth his best smile.
Not the most handsome man she'd ever met, she
admitted, but still he had something . . . special.
She tried again and again to remember they worked
together. Alex, however, had shown himself with
such loyalty and conviction for the clinic, a place
where he made very little money compared to what
most doctors made, that she couldn't help but want
to see him succeed. The whole reason she'd seen to
it he had the opportunity to be here.

It had nothing to do with him being charming
and funny. Nothing at all.

"Beth," Dina asked, "do you still strictly not date
people with whom you work?"

Alex, seated between the two women wondered
if he were in danger. Dina suddenly turned Glenn
Close on him, but he confessed to himself his interest didn't lie with her anyway.

He contained a grin. It remained on his boss.
Who would be a hard nut to crack, to say the least.

He knew he shouldn't be looking at her as a man looks at a woman. She was his boss, for goodness sake. His supervisor, his superior, his manager, his administrator, yes she was all those things. But, this woman had somehow captured his attention and he just had to see where it could lead.

Anyhow, someone had seen to it he attended this conference and for some reason, he suspected Ms. Chambers was the ally.

The conference chairperson tapped the microphone and introduced the luncheon speaker. Dina tried to make conversation throughout the lecture, but Alex only nodded, hoping to quiet her.

After the speech ended, Dina was called to another table by her supervisor. Before she left him, she wrote her home number on the back of her business card. "Let me know if you're ever in Nashville."

He winked. "I will." Relief flooded him. She'd become a little too possessive based on only a short talk after a session they had both attended.

When he turned to talk to Beth, she too had slipped away. A moment ago, he'd had two beautiful women surrounding him. Now he stood alone.

He sighed, *The story of my life.*

The Saturday night banquet and reception boasted one of the most acclaimed speakers in the Kentucky Hospital and Medical Management

Association. Beth had looked forward to this the entire weekend.

As she slipped on her earrings, she looked in the mirror. *Not bad, Chambers. Not bad at all.* She never looked at herself as anything but a business-woman. But tonight, she wanted to look and feel good. Not that anything could quite top the feeling she had when Alex Price had spoken her name.

She dropped her makeup brush in the sink. The man's memory made her jittery. Everything about him, his compassion, his humor, his aftershave, made her want to get closer. She didn't like that. In fact, she was too old for this type of thing. She'd made her decision years ago. Much like Scarlet O'Hara, she'd never be poor again. She'd worked too hard to get where she was to throw it all away on a doctor who had no idea what the value of money in today's world meant.

Not that she lusted after money, but on the other side of the coin, she wouldn't wear another second-hand piece of clothing as long as she lived.

Which brought her back to the mirror. She wore a deep green cocktail dress that fell right above her knee. Her jewelry, all real fourteen carat gold, con-sisted of earrings, a bracelet, watch, and necklace that rested perfectly on the high bodice of the dress.

She'd looked high and low for just this dress, paying top price for it.

After one last look in the mirror, she decided her

reflection was presentable and turned out the bathroom light.

Dina met her at the elevator, decked out in a little black dress. "Where did Alex get to after I left?"

"I wouldn't know, Dina, I went straight to my next workshop."

Dina nodded as if she didn't believe Beth. What Dina didn't know was that Beth could care less what she thought.

When the doors opened on the appropriate floor, Beth exited before Dina had a chance to ask more questions. She didn't really pay much heed to some of the men she knew from past conferences asking her where she would be seated, or complimenting her hair, pulled onto the top of her head in a neat French twist.

A pressure at the small of her back told her someone had joined her in her trek towards the Colonial Hall. Without turning, she knew it was Alex Price.

"I'm just here for protection," his whispered words sent a chill down her spine.

"Protection from what?" It was the only thing she could think to say.

"Every other man here who sees you in this dress. You are definitely the belle of the ball."

Though she didn't know why, she allowed him to guide her toward the appetizer tables and even get her a cup of punch.

"I don't think I really need protection, Alex. I've

been to conferences. I always get away unscathed."
She matched his tone of voice, intimate and low.

"I know. But since I'm here, I'd really like the
job. Anyway, you can protect me, as well," he cast a
sidelong glance toward the end of the room where
Dina trolled for men.

She smiled, knowingly. "Planning a move to
Nashville?"

He filled a plate with goodies from the table.
"Not in this lifetime. But, for some reason, Ms.
Kimball must think so. I only talked to her for
a few minutes before you arrived at the table today."

He offered the plate to her and she took a small
cucumber sandwich from it. The hors d'oeuvre
melted in her mouth and she picked up a plate so
she could get more.

Alex placed his lips near her ear. "I think we
should think about complete safety this evening.
You can save me from Ms. Kimball, and I'll make
sure you make it to your room."

"I don't need a knight, Alex."

"Think of it as helping me, then. Because here
she comes."

In four-inch heels and the proverbial little black
dress, little being an operative word of description,
Dina slinked up to Alex and hugged him. "You look
great this evening."

"One nice thing about being a man is a suit is a

suit. You ladies are the ones who wonder what to wear."

"Beth, I'm sure you won't mind if I steal Alex for the night." Dina linked an arm through Alex's protectively.

Beth now became the uninvited. It only took a second to understand what Alex needed from her. Had they both been asked to the table, Beth probably would have accepted the invitation and watched him squirm. Dina, however, had made it clear Beth's presence wasn't requested.

"Actually, Alex and I have decided to make this a working dinner. I'm sorry, but we need to discuss some things and need a little privacy."

Dina's face changed from tolerance to anger. "You were always the one who preached against getting involved with people on the job."

Alex jumped into the fire. "If it makes you feel any better, Dina, I'm not paying tonight."

Beth almost laughed. Of course he wasn't paying, the dinner was part of the conference.

In a whine Dina asked, "Would you rather have a business dinner with her than to spend time with me, Alex?"

"You know, I think I would. If you'll excuse us." Alex led Beth through the crowd and found a table near the wall. There were already a few people sitting there, but the seats they chose were out of the major swarm of attendees.

Beth took a drink of her water after they sat down. "You know, that was about to get real ugly. I'd seen Dina set her mind on men before but not like that."

"Honestly, I'm not flattered. I didn't do anything but talk to her. I've given you a lot more attention."

She shouldn't have taken that as a compliment, but she did. She shouldn't want his attention, but she couldn't seem to help herself. "You realize you'll really have to sit with me now, or she'll say something."

He lifted his tea glass in the air, like a toast. "I'm exactly where I want to be."

She lifted her glass in return, with a smile. *Dangerous territory, Beth. Don't let this guy take your eye off the prize.*

It all had the feel of a first date. The ambiance of not really knowing how to act or what to say. The shyness when someone asked how long they'd been together. At two separate times they were asked if they were married. Someone else commented on what a handsome couple they made.

Alex took all the questions in stride. Short answers but big smiles. She thought he liked it.

By the time dinner was over and the speaker had finished what had probably been a wonderful and educated view on keeping down the cost of healthcare, all Beth wondered is if Alex would want to attend the dance offered afterward.

Not that she liked to dance. But, he'd have reason

to hold her close and the thought kept her in a constant state of anticipation.

As people milled around, Alex led Beth wordlessly into the dance area at the far end of the room and took her in his arms.

She moved close to him as if they were meant to be there for this very reason, and Trentville Memorial Hospital didn't even exist. The lights were dim and the music soft, as he took the appropriate steps and she followed.

Then, just before the music ended, Alex placed his lips on hers with a kiss so sweet, her eyes misted.

"Don't be angry," he whispered against her ear just before the song ended.

But, when they pulled away from each other, Beth became so uncomfortable with the situation, she softly told him, "I have to get back to my room. I'm leaving early."

"Let me walk you back."

"No."

He looked dejected. "Because I kissed you."

"No. Yes. I'm not sure." She left him then without another word.

Alex stood looking after her. Inside that façade of business and money was a heart. He'd almost found it. Almost.

Sunday afternoon she dressed in a sweater and jeans, pulled her hair into a ponytail and packed her suitcases. The dress she'd worn last night still smelled of the party. Alex's cologne and . . . well, that was the most of it. She held it close to her face for a moment. The kiss they'd shared, so pure and perfect and so inappropriate. She shook her head and threw the dress into the dirty clothes bag. This line of thought wouldn't take her anywhere.

She would not be taken advantage of. Not again, she'd been down that trail in the past. After leaving a tip for the maid, she picked up her suitcases and left the room.

The trip had been worthwhile, but her emotions got in the way, and that didn't work. Definitely not the way she liked her life. All simple and based on tangible items and logic, that's how she wanted it. Even her aunt's cameo, which she wore on a chain no one ever saw, was a neat little reminder of her past. Her aunt's devotion to her was all she had growing up. No money or clothes and sometimes, they had little food. But, she had been loved. Was it precious to her? More so than anything else she owned. That didn't make it any less a cheap, plastic piece of costume jewelry.

In the parking garage, she saw Alex get into a car that she couldn't believe belonged to a doctor. She stopped momentarily, for no reason more than to say hello. That's what she told herself at least. "So, you're ready to go, I see."

"Yep. I'm ready. You want to stop for breakfast somewhere? I'll buy."

Good chance to prove to herself she had no feelings for this man. "Sure, why not?"

"I'll meet you at the restaurant across the street."

"Okay."

A few moments later, they sat with menus in hand, deciding between eggs and pancakes. Beth, just a little off-kilter, ordered then took a large gulp of her water.

He wasted no time. "Want to tell me why you weren't at all surprised to see me at this thing?"

Beth choked on her water. Literally. She ran from the table to the ladies restroom. It took several moments for her to recoup not only her gag reflex but what was she going to say to him. She hadn't thought to act shocked when she saw him; he had to know that she was behind the trip.

That was okay, she justified. It was fine. She had it all covered, at least in her mind, when she rejoined him at the table.

"Are you all right?"

"I'm fine. I'm so sorry. I took too big a drink of my water, and it went down wrong. Believe it or not, I'm still hungry." Which was good, because her pancakes sat in front her.

He wore his metal-framed glasses, like she'd seen him her first day of work. Instead of the charming playboy, he looked more a serious professional, if one could get past the twinkle in his blue eyes. "Before you take a bite, and choke to death, will you answer my question?"

She quickly took a bite and chewed. "What question?" She asked around her food.

He pulled his glasses down to look over them. "You're avoiding something, aren't you Ms. Chambers?"

"Why are you wearing glasses?"

He pushed them back up on his nose. "I lost a contact this morning."

"Lost it? How?"

"Down the drain."

She shrugged. Sounded reasonable. She took another bite. Best pancakes she'd had in months. Of course, since she usually ate a protein bar in the morning, they were the first pancakes she'd had in months.

"Let's go back to why you got so choked up." He finally picked up his own fork and took a bite of his eggs.

"I told you—"

"I know what you *told* me. You knew I'd be here, didn't you?"

"I suspected that you would be on top of things and come. That's all. There were good tracks here for people who run clinics like yours."

"And clinics like mine can't afford to send me to conferences like this. I think you were the one who financed this whole thing. Through the hospital, sure, but you did it all the same."

"I don't think Mr. Luft would have allowed you to come, Dr. Price. Not at all."

"Is that an admission or an effort to avoid the question?"

She didn't answer.

Alex put his fork down, but before he sipped his juice, he said, "I believe you about the hospital. Gordon Luft doesn't care about anything but the bottom line."

"It makes him successful," she argued.

"It makes him hate a clinic set up to help those less fortunate."

"He has pictures in his office. He drives a beautiful car, owns a gorgeous house, and has kept the hospital in the black at a time when many are not."

"Whoever dies with the most toys is not the most successful person, Beth. You'd do good to remember that."

She stiffened. "Don't preach to me about things you know nothing about."

He remained quiet throughout the rest of the meal. In fact, neither said more than "pass the salt" the entire time.

The waitress gave Alex the ticket, but Beth grabbed it from him. "I'll take care of it."

He eyed her a long moment. "You're on an expense account for this, so sure, I'll let you handle it." He gave her the check. "See ya back at the ranch." With that he saluted and walked away.

She paid the bill and walked to her car. Next to it, Alex had the hood of his own green bomb in the air.

She approached him. "Everything okay?"

He wiped his hands on a rag. "It's probably the water pump. At least, from the noise it made, I think it is."

"You'll never find a place open on a Sunday. You'd be better off to let someone tow it to their garage and keep it until you can get back up here."

He nodded. "Don't worry about me, I'll get the auto club to help me out with the towing and handle a rental for me."

The words were out of her mouth before she thought. "There's no reason for you to rent a car when I'm going right through Ft. White."

"How do you know where I live?"

She grinned in an effort to hide the fact she'd been curious about him. "I know lots of things about my department heads."

He pulled out his cell phone and called the auto club. Within the half hour they were on their way home.

The trip lay before them and they had two goals: One, to get home. And two, to not kill each other in the next three hours.

Chapter Three

The first thirty minutes of the ride was an uncomfortable silence interrupted only by a clumsily stated comment regarding minute things including the weather, the terrain, the horse farms they passed, and other subjects of disinterest. Those safe items that wouldn't start an argument, be taken wrong, or just cause the atmosphere to be any more strained than it was.

Finally, Beth looked at him and said, "You know, Dr. Price, you've got my attention, whether I like it or not, for the next two and a half hours. You may as well plead the case of the clinic while you have the chance."

With a sidelong glance, he said, "I don't know, Ms. Chambers. You got your name brands on from your high-priced running shoes to your hundred dollar sunglasses. I'm not sure you'd understand where I'm coming from."

He expected a rise from her; instead she offered him a sad smile. "Think I always dressed this way?"

"I can see you in high school. Voted the girl most likely to succeed. Or maybe best dressed."

"If only." She shook her head as if to erase bad memories, then sighed. "You remember that girl in every high school the kids made fun of because she dressed from the secondhand shop?"

He couldn't hide his surprise. "You were that girl in your school?"

She nodded. "One day, a girl said to me she used to have a dress like mine. It *was* hers."

"Did you die from embarrassment?"

"I got over it. I worked my way through college along with grants and scholarships."

"I admit it, I'm surprised."

"That I don't come from old money?"

"That you shared that information with me."

They fell into a long silence.

He fidgeted and moved in the seat. "Are we there yet?"

She laughed. "No, not yet. You've got over two more hours, so tell me about the clinic."

"Well, okay. At least it won't be as silent as death in here." He paused then started his story. "About three years ago, Trentville Memorial was in really bad financial shape. They had everything they needed to work out their problems. Good staff. Plenty of beds. All the things to make a good facility were there. But, people passed us up to go into Fort White for medical care."

"Where were you when all this happened?" She signaled to change lanes.

"I had just passed my boards and worked in the ER."

"So, at this point, there was no clinic?"

"No. The board did some investigating. They found that many of the specialists who came in from Fort White to take local appointments weren't using our hospital. Instead, they'd take their patients with them to Fort White for special treatments or testing."

"That makes sense. Ft. White is larger. They already have their centers set up. Did the hospital offer the doctors anything?"

"Free lunch." He chuckled.

She glanced at him. "No, really. Usually this situation calls for some drastic measures. Free rent or paying to keep certain diagnostic testing at Memorial."

"The board did some of those things. The doctors started referring at least some patients and procedures to the hospital. That's when I stepped in and upset some people."

"Did you bring the pig?" She laughed.

"Nothing so reasonable. I called an old pal of mine from med school and that's when we started the pet therapy on the peds wing."

"I see. That's why you're so concerned about that department."

He pointed at her like a teacher would a student who just gave a correct answer. "That would be the reason. But you need to consider, we're the only hospital for a hundred miles in any direction that uses pet therapy in acute care facilities, *and* it's working." He briefly detailed a couple of cases where having the pets available had turned a critically ill child around, smiling at the success of his pet project.

He had a nice smile. No wonder women fell so hard for this guy and he could get them to do his bidding without asking. Most men couldn't pull off the little boy with a secret look, but Alex Price did it extremely well.

She came back from Planet Smile and asked, "And, how does the clinic fit into all this?"

"I had this idea for a clinic for the uninsured, or low income citizens."

"Which the board bought?"

"Which the newspaper got wind of. The resulting publicity pretty much forced the hospital to go along with it."

"So you took the power of decision out of the

board's hands. Now I know why Luft hates you. My next question is, who were you dating at the paper?"

In a playful tone he told her, "I resent that."

"But, you didn't answer it, so it tells me there was someone." She tried to hide a grin.

"I did use my powers of persuasions to get some help on this, that's all I'll admit to."

With a trace of laughter in her voice, she answered, "I'm sure you did."

By the time he finished telling her more about the clinic, an hour had gone by. He'd fought a good fight, with hope in his voice and a determination to keep to his convictions, Beth found him to be less the manipulative jokester and more a dedicated physician.

Her hands gripped the steering wheel. "I think you should know I had a board member, other than Luft, ask me about the clinic."

"It wasn't a positive thing, was it?"

"No. The board is not convinced it was a good idea in the beginning."

"What do *you* think?"

She didn't want to give him an answer that was hurtful, but she wouldn't lie either. "I haven't been here long enough to make an informed decision."

"And the pet therapy?"

"I won't discuss another department with you." She turned on the supervisor tone.

"Fair enough."

A state trooper fell in behind Beth and started flashing blue lights. Alex turned and glanced behind them then flashed Beth a look of disbelief.

"How fast were you going?"

She signaled and pulled the car onto the shoulder. "I didn't pay any attention, it looks like I was doing over eighty."

His face scrunched. "Not good."

"Thank you for your enlightening comment."

She rolled her down window. "May I help you?" She asked the female officer.

"License, registration, and proof of insurance, please." The woman looked masculine in her hat and uniform, but there was something in her voice that led Beth to believe she'd kept enough femininity about her.

The trooper looked at the articles she'd asked for. "Do you know how fast you were going, Miss Chambers?"

"I'm not sure." Not a total lie, since she hadn't been watching the speedometer.

"Eighty-three in a sixty-five mile per hour speed zone. That's at least fifteen miles over the speed limit. I not only have you for speeding, but I can write you a ticket for reckless driving as well. I'll be right back." The trooper walked to her car.

Alex appeared fidgety. "Do you realize the trouble you're in? They could impound the car on a reckless driving charge, and I need to work the ER tonight."

"You're supposed to be the salesman of the team. You do something." She fired back, embarrassed at having been pulled over.

"Fine." He opened his door. "I'll be right back."

He walked casually towards the other car, as the trooper stepped out of hers. With both hands where she could see them, he approached her. Beth heard the entire conversation through her open window.

"I know my friend was speeding, but the truth is we are on our way back to the hospital where we work."

"Really no excuse, Mr . . ."

"Actually, it's *Dr.* Price. I'm on emergency room duty tonight and this lady, who's my boss by the way, is just trying to get me there. That's all. We were at a seminar in Lexington. I'm sure you don't normally cut anyone a break, but really, we're just trying to get back in time."

"I'm sorry," her voice softened, obviously he had turned on a charm Beth couldn't see from her rearview mirror, "but we have laws."

"I understand. And, those laws are to protect people. I'm in the same business. Protecting people, helping people, it's all the same thing."

"Yeah, but you make a whole lot more money—"

"I bet I don't make more money than you do."

Sarcasm dripped from her lips. "I'm so sure, Doctor."

"No, really. I run a clinic at the hospital for uninsured people and work the ER. Which brings me back to why we were speeding. I'm due in the ER in three hours."

The woman wavered. "She *was* doing over fifteen miles over the speed limit."

"To get me, to work on time. If you give her the ticket, I'll have to pay it, just to be fair to her."

"Looks like, with that car, she could afford her own ticket." The officer eyed the luxury model Beth had saved three years to buy.

"I know. I know. But, looks *can* be deceiving."

There it was again, the woman's hesitation. He'd take advantage of that. Beth knew it. "I'll tell you what, Doc. *You* drive out of Kentucky, per the speed limit, and I'll let her get away with a warning."

Beth saw his smile in the mirror. Sweet and charming, she wanted to throw up. "How can I thank you?"

She removed her hat and handed him something. "Here's my card, look me up the next time you're in my neck of the woods."

Without the hat, the woman was about their age and quite attractive. Alex smiled. "You got it."

He went to the driver's side of the car. "I'll drive from here."

Disgust laced her tone. "I don't think—"

His voice held a firmness she'd never heard before. "Unless you want your insurance rates to go sky high, I'll drive from here."

"Fine." She huffed and got out of the car, walking around it, as the trooper pulled onto the interstate. "I can't believe you just talked your way out of that. I can't believe you . . . I just can't believe *you*." She got in the passenger's side and slammed her door.

He didn't pull out into traffic; instead he faced her. "A thank you would be nice, you know."

"I have a problem with someone flirting his way out of any situation."

"You call that flirting?"

"Didn't she give you her card?"

"Did you hear me ask for it?"

"Not exactly—"

"Listen, Beth, when I flirt, you'll know it. I'm a great flirt." He looked forward, then started the car with a frustrated grunt and an exaggerated movement.

"If that wasn't flirting, I don't know what is." She sat in her seat, her arms crossed over her chest. She tried to ignore the niggling reminders of the times she'd talked herself out of speeding tickets with male officers. *This* was different, somehow. And she refused to acknowledge just how.

He put the car in drive, then back into park. He faced her again. "You wouldn't know flirting. I'd say you've never batted those big green eyes. You've never learned how to use your feminine wiles, have you?"

"I . . . I—" she sputtered.

"Just as I thought. You're not mad at me for flirting, you're mad because you can't." This time when he faced towards the front, he put the car in drive and pulled onto the interstate.

"I can too flirt!"

"I doubt it." His voice held that totally infuriating male tone of superiority.

"No, really, I can." Why was it so important for this man to know she could do something so childish?

"I don't believe you even know what it is. You called my conversation back there flirting. Had that been a man, how would you have handled it?"

If just to prove a point she proudly announced, "I'd have paid the ticket."

"Oh, yeah. You'd do the noble thing, right? No. You'd do what you had to do because you just don't have the people skills to get around it."

"How dare you speak to me like that? I have people skills. I just don't manipulate people the way you do."

"When have you ever seen me manipulate anyone?"

"The first time we met! What was it you said to Mona the volunteer when she offered to take Joey to the peds wing?" She mimicked him, "That's why you get the pink jacket."

"That is *not* manipulation. It's people skills."

"Use those skills to remember I'm your supervisor."

"Perfect example. Throw your weight around." He used a falsetto voice, "I'm your supervisor." Shaking his head, he continued, "I have a contract, so unless you want to buy me out, I'll be where I always am."

"You know, Alex, you brag about how you get around people, but you don't explain why you have to do these things to begin with. Are you a mess-up looking for a way out?"

Alex got extremely quiet for a long moment. Beth thought that, like he'd done, she'd gone too far.

"Actually, I'm the oldest of three children. An average Joe kind of guy whose sisters are so beautiful they stop traffic. You learn to use what you have."

She almost laughed. "I don't believe this. You see yourself as the funny one."

He braked as the car beside him went by, then abruptly changed lanes to pass the one in front of him. "What's that supposed to mean?"

"It means you don't know that you're good-looking because your sisters out-shined you growing up."

"They didn't purposefully do anything. They're great people—"

"I don't doubt it one bit. Tessa appeared to be very nice. It's just you don't see yourself the way others see you, so you overcompensate to try to get people to like you, no—" she held a finger up for emphasis. "It's to get attention. You need everyone to look at you and say," she used a false baritone voice, "that Alex Price is a great guy."

She waited for his response.

He continued to drive.

After a long few moments, she looked forward and not at him.

In the tense atmosphere, he still did not respond. She wanted to beg him to argue his point. But, she didn't.

Time passed. He said nothing.

After what seemed like hours, but couldn't have been more than a few minutes he took a deep breath. "Can we just close this subject and move on to something else?"

She'd hit a nerve. Guilt engulfed her. "That's fine."

Beth decided to use the time for something more than thinking about how uncomfortable the mood was, and took her briefcase from the backseat. Time passed as she went over certain reports.

He never said a word.

After almost an hour, he told her, "We need gas."

"That's fine." She looked up from her papers. "Just pull off anywhere."

A few moments later, she found herself outside a gas station with a convenience store. Alex pumped and paid for the gas. She didn't get out of the car.

He got back in and fastened his seat belt to find her in the backseat working on her laptop.

"Are you back already?" Disappointed it hadn't taken longer, as she was getting some work done.

"It only takes a few minutes to do all the necessities. Which, by the way, aren't you going to the restroom? We have at least another hour before we get home."

"Don't have to go. And, if you don't mind, I can navigate my laptop better back here. Is that okay?"

He used the buttons on his door to push the seat up beside him to give her more legroom. "Not at all . . . Miss Daisy. Are you sure about the restroom? I'd hate to have to stop again."

She snickered. "I'll be fine. I promise, you won't have to."

Once they were back on the road and Beth became engaged in her work, she realized something.

She should have taken his advice and gone to the restroom.

She ignored it.

Then, she became conscious that it was too much to ignore. So she recognized it, but she told herself she could hold it, after all, she was a big girl now.

"We're not far from home," Alex told her, "but you know, it would be a lot quicker for me if we stopped to see the new baby on our way in."

"Does your sister live closer than you do?"

"Oh, yeah. She's not only on the north side, but by the time we get through the construction sites downtown, it could add another forty-five minutes to our drive."

She wouldn't last that long. "Well, I know you want to see the baby." She wondered; could he see her eyeballs floating in her head?

His voice was full of appreciation. "It means a lot to me to get to see Cole. I feel as if I've been away forever."

He didn't know that at that moment she used her people skills to get what she wanted. "Not at all."

And, she wouldn't tell him, either.

The driveway at his sister's house was full of cars. She counted them and came up with four.

Inside, she tried to get through explanations of why she was there and introductions, but finally just asked if she could use the restroom and headed there, post haste.

Words couldn't describe her relief once she got there and finished her chore. She washed her hands, checked her hair and makeup in the mirror, and unlocked the door.

When she opened it, Alex stood outside leaning against the wall. "You okay?"

She replied, "I'm fine."

He didn't try to hide the smirk. "You seemed . . . *preoccupied* when meeting my family."

"No, I'm fine, really." She walked past him, determined not to admit he'd been right about the restroom break.

"It *is* your car. I believe I could have stopped."

She turned to face him. "Was it *that* obvious?"

"I thought so. You asked about the bathroom three times in as many minutes."

She caught the front of his shirt in her hand in a mock threat. "Don't you ever tell anyone about this."

He held up his hands as if surrendering.. "I won't, please don't hurt me."

"Good. Let me try honing my people skills on your family. Especially since I seem to have made a bad first impression."

He looked down at her, blue eyes full of mischief. "You made a fine first impression. I think I was the only one who knew you were, shall we say, anxious?"

"That's the word. Meeting your family was like going through an obstacle course to get here." She nodded toward the restroom.

He kissed her. She hadn't expected it. She didn't realize what he did until it was done. He tasted good, too. Cinnamon candy, from his trip to the convenience store added to his flavor.

His voice husky, he told her, "Let's get down to the den, Mom brought fudge."

In the den, Joey made his preference known by

settling at her feet. Occasionally, he would lick her knee or ankle. When Alex, who'd sat beside her, got up for a soft drink, Joey climbed on the couch and laid his head in her lap.

"What in the world is Joey doing?" Michael Sommers watched as his adoptive child grunted and snorted for Beth.

Danni, holding the baby, giggled. "I feel like a mother going through her child's first crush."

Beth rubbed his tummy most of the time they were there.

They stayed almost two hours. When she got up to leave, Joey squealed and ran around the room. He'd always stop at Beth's feet, but when someone tried to grab him, start all over again. Finally, Michael, Danni's husband, had to put him in the yard to keep him from hurting himself.

His family had been not only friendly but also kind. In the end, Beth found herself promising to come to dinner, along with Alex, the next week. Alex took Beth's hand and led her to the door. They said their goodbyes and got in the car.

After leaving Danni's place, they started for Alex's apartment.

"I don't date people with whom I work." She blurted totally out of context of the conversation they'd been having about the fudge.

"I know. You've made that clear."

"Then why did you kiss me, of all things?"

He shrugged. "Why not?"

She pushed him further, but he didn't answer her questions. She finally gave up.

They got downtown within thirty minutes. A good time, figuring all the orange drums scattered everywhere and lanes that were closed.

He drove and pulled the car into the parking garage of his building.

She didn't even attempt to hide her shock. "You live *here?*"

Chapter Four

He opened his door. But before he got out he looked at her. "Guilty as charged."

She got out of the car as well. "With all your noble talk of helping those without insurance and those who can't afford decent health care."

Mixed emotions crossed his handsome face. "Which means?"

"You treat me like I'm some sort of princess because I wear decent clothing, and you live in one of the most upscale buildings in the city." She didn't exaggerate. The building was an old warehouse, several stories high, which had been remodeled into huge condominiums. Though Beth had never seen one, she'd read they were as large as half a floor of the building. That had to be thirty-five hundred square feet.

"It's a long story. I never meant to buy an apartment, much less an upscale one, as you say."

"I've got the time, it's only four o'clock."

He paused as if in the middle of making a decision. "You know," he swung his luggage from the trunk, "I'm just not in the mood to tell you any more of my life story. You're not really interested in me anyway. Remember? So, get in your car, and I'll go up and get some rest before work tonight."

For some reason, Beth felt guilty. "I didn't mean to offend you."

His voice softened, "You didn't really. I just need some rest and time to think." He closed the trunk lid. "I think you should contemplate the things that happened this weekend. Not the workshops. Last night and today."

She unwillingly moved closer. "I will. But, I can tell you the answer will always be the same."

"I don't think that it's the answer you should worry about. I think it's the question." He arched a brow.

"Just state your point, Alex. Quit playing your games."

"Okay." He dropped his suitcase and travel bag to the concrete floor. "Here it is, your answer is you don't get involved with coworkers, employees, the list goes on. But, the real question is could you fall in love with me?"

She gasped. "In love? You think that two kisses could make me fall in love?"

He took her in his arms. He stared at her a long moment, she wanted to run away, but was too befuddled to move. His blue gaze poured over her eyes and lips.

She couldn't breathe, which made her a bit light-headed.

Then he released her, with a devastatingly handsome smile.

Cold disappointment and confusion washed over her. She didn't want complications. She didn't want to get involved with another man at work. But, she wanted the way his kisses made her feel.

That was new for her.

"Now, ask the question. But be careful, princess, because I don't think you'll like the answer." He winked at her.

Adrenaline rose from her toes and moved all the way to the top of her head. Her stomach hurt and anger gripped her like a vice. "How dare you?"

He didn't answer. He just walked away, his gear in hand.

"Did you hear me? How dare you speak to me like that? Who do you think you are?"

He boarded the elevator, more of a storage or

freight lift, and she followed suit, not stopping to take a breath.

"I am your supervisor and contract or not, I can have you dismissed with just cause."

The elevator continued its slow passage by each floor as her tirade continued.

"You may think you have all the answers and all the questions. But, you know nothing about me. Nothing. I am not to be manhandled again, Dr. Price. I mean that. You are to never lay another finger on me. Is that clear?"

"Crystal." His tone held no emotion.

"You will never be allowed in my office alone. Ever. You have something to say to me, put it in a memo. Do you understand?" She heard the bitter edge of anger in her voice.

"Yes."

The elevator stopped and Alex opened the gate. The door he unlocked was wide, as if it had once been used for storage of something very large. However, when it was opened, the door revealed a massive loft-style apartment. Beautiful, she acknowledged, but sparse in furniture or any other type of accessory.

He stepped inside, carrying his luggage across the threshold with him. "You coming in?" He'd been completely calm since she'd lit into him downstairs.

"I am not! Haven't you heard a word I said?"

"Yes, I did. Thank you for sharing your thoughts with me. Now, if you don't mind of course, I'm going to bed for a while. I drove most of the way back, and I'm really on at the emergency room tonight."

She stuttered, but no words came out of her mouth.

"The red button is down. Goodnight." He gently pulled the bay door closed.

For a long moment, Beth stood where she was. Shaking her head, trying to figure out how she'd lost control, she took a couple of steps to the button and pushed it. The elevator started its slow trek back down.

In love, indeed! She'd show him. She would. She just wasn't sure how at this moment, but it would come to her.

Eventually.

"If you think I'm keeping him here, you're wrong, counselor." Alex spoke to his brother-in-law, Michael, Danni's husband.

He stood in front of Alex, looking a little blurry since Alex neither had on his glasses nor had in his contacts. "Please, Alex. Joey's become so jealous. After you and your friend left this afternoon, he started pulling the baby's diapers from the little hanging thingy that Danni keeps them in. Then he chewed on them. After that, he turned over the diaper pail and scattered it all over the nursery. And Danni has cried all evening. Between the baby not sleeping, and Joey acting up, she's a mess."

Alex looked down at the pig perched at Michael's side, and for the life of him thought the creature looked pleased with himself.

Alex thought about Danni, in a hormone frenzy with all this going on around her. "What about Tessa?"

"She kept him the last time."

That was too true. She'd had a royal time with him. Of course, she got a husband out of all that.

"Mike, I'm really not trying to be difficult, but what will I do with him? I work odd hours." He checked his watch. "In fact, I'm supposed to be at work in just a couple of hours."

"During the nights, he rests, just like most animals. During the days, he usually sleeps if no one is at home."

Alex sighed. "And Danni is upset?"

"Very."

"Okay, I'll keep the varmint. But, don't think you won't owe me and big in some way in the future."

Michael dropped the large overnight bag that held Joey's food and other items of interest in it. After he left, Joey sniffed at every nook and cranny of the apartment.

Alex went to bed where Joey soon followed and laid down on the floor beside him.

He was crazy to take the animal in, but for Danni he'd do it. The truth had never been clearer; those sisters of his could get him to do anything.

Rhoda put her feet on Beth's coffee table. "I think this has been coming since the pig tripped you." She sipped a drink and made a face that insured it held her current fascination, vinegar. Beth made a note to get whatever she drank in the apartment herself.

"I can't believe he has the nerve to even look at me after the way he pawed me."

"Pawed you? Sounds like you enjoyed it!" Rhoda's voice held humor.

"I did not! I should sue him for sexual harassment."

"You know, Beth, if you'd worry about your heart the way you worry about your job. Or, the past."

"I can only say that I'm not putting myself in another man-at-work situation."

Rhoda became quiet but intently studied Beth. Shaking her head as if she'd finished reading a sentence she didn't understand, Rhoda sat down on the sofa. "I really want to tell you something. Your Dr. Price knows you. He knows your intentions and he's still interested. I think you're lucky."

"Lucky? Are you crazy? I'm business. There's nothing wrong with that. He thinks he has people skills, but he's just all charm and flirting."

"But, that may be just what the doctor ordered." She stood. "I really need to go."

"Are you upset because I won't date the doctor?"

"Not really. Honestly, though, I wish you'd learn to follow your heart and really live."

"I found out that leads only to hurt. Not a road I wish to travel again, thank you very much."

Rhoda sighed as she opened the door. "I wish you could forget Laurence County Health Care, Frank Blair, and how you left that job because of him. I wish you could just settle in where you are, make friends, and fall in love with this Dr. Nice Guy."

Beth stood near the open door. "You ask too much. Way too much."

Mist filled the older woman's eyes. "Your happiness is too much to ask?"

Beth gestured to the living area in which they stood. *"This* is my happiness, not depending on anyone but me. Having the things that some people only dream of, *that* brings me happiness. Knowing I can make my own way, and it's *more* than survival. What more could I ask for?"

"Friends other than me, aka the crazy old woman next door. Someone your age who goes to movies with you and shops with you and does the things your age group does."

Beth huffed and started to speak, but Rhoda held up a hand to stop her. "And love, honey. Some nice guy to come home to at night. Kids. Who's going to keep you company in your old age?"

"I'll buy a dog." The words weren't even convincing to Beth's own ears. A pot-bellied pig immediately took the place of a small puppy in her mind.

"Think about what I'm saying, baby. Just think." Rhoda was gone.

Beth closed the door and hoped she'd quit thinking about what Rhoda said, especially the part about Alex Price. She didn't want a man like him. He found no interest in upwardly mobile ambitions.

After she straightened the room one last time, Beth hit the shower. She'd had a hard day and her neighbor's revelations hadn't helped her one bit.

"Hey, Alex!"

He turned to see Darlene Thompson moving quickly toward him on the walkway outside the hospital.

"Hey, lady! What's up?" The wind tore at their coats. Last night, December had truly set in and the temperatures proved it.

"Can we talk a second? I need to ask you something."

"Sure, but you look pretty serious and I'm not in that mode right now."

She shook her head as he followed her into the side entrance to the hospital. They stepped into the hospital's small chapel and, finding it empty, sat in the back pew.

"What brings you away from the zoo?" Alex smiled. He only called it that because Luft hated it and that was his name for the pet therapy she did.

For a long moment, Darlene appeared shy. "You are probably going to laugh at this."

"Probably." He gave her a friendly nudge on the shoulder. "So, give it to me straight. What's going on?"

"It's about your pig."

A feeling of dread moved its way into Alex's stomach. "My pig?"

"It's a long story. You remember Amber?"

"The little girl with the burn scar? Yeah, I do. She's precious. Is she okay? Did Joey hurt her?"

"Just the opposite. Ever since you had him upstairs, she's been asking for him. He was so loving with her that she wants to see him again. Do you think we could borrow him for a week or so?"

"I'll see what I can do." Alex smiled to himself more than at Darlene. *Pig problem: stamp it solved!*

Beth took a few days to work from home. She needed some time to assimilate the information she'd gotten in Lexington as well as time to . . . no, not true. She didn't need time to get the courage to face Dr. Price. That had nothing to do with her decision.

While she was out she gave Lucy the days off, forwarded most of her calls, answered all her mail and email, and interviewed some assistants. All in all the extra two days had been quite productive.

Back at work, Lucy caught her putting the key in the lock.

"Excuse me, Miss," Lucy told her as she approached Beth, "Miss Shults wouldn't like you going into her office without her knowledge."

Beth sighed. A deep sigh. One that would have spoken volumes to someone who lived on planet Earth. "Lucy, this is *my* office. I'm Ms. Chambers, remember?"

Lucy shook her head from side to side. "Well, *Ms. Chambers*, I'm sure Miss Shults won't appreciate you taking over her office. From what I've met of the woman, she'll probably be quite upset."

Once Beth had turned the key and unlocked the door, she turned back to her secretary. "Lucy, when Miss Shults gets here, you can tell her I'm inside and we'll see if she gets upset."

"It's your job. I definitely wouldn't take a chance like that. You know what they call her."

Interest piqued, Beth asked, "What is that?"

Lucy leaned forward and whispered, "The Dragon Lady."

Enough was enough. "You wait on the Dragon Lady then, and see if she shows for work today."

"I most certainly will. And if she does, you'll be looking for new employment. I'll tell Mr. Luft too."

"I hope you do."

Beth entered the office and closed the door. She emailed her department heads to let them know she was in the office and warned them to call her directly before visiting her. Lucy would stop them for sure.

In the midst of dictating a letter, Beth noticed the door open a bit. She clicked off the recorder and turned to see Alex standing in the entrance, his arm around Lucy's shoulders. The older lady had a perplexed if not perturbed expression on her face, although, like every other female in the place, she preened at his attention.

Alex patted Lucy's arm. "See, I told you it was Ms. Chambers. She emailed me. That's how I knew."

"How did she get the mail out of her office without coming by me?"

Beth wanted to scream. She opened her mouth to explain the ins and outs of computer technology to Lucy but refrained when Alex slightly shook his head.

"It's a long story. But, it's okay to let me in and I'll talk to Mr. Luft about Miss Shults, okay?"

He smoothly pivoted Lucy in the direction of the reception desk. "Oh, Dr. Kennedy, you're so kind. Thank you." With a chilly nod to Beth, the secretary exited.

Alex's face fell. Apparently, he thought he'd

reached some sort of headway with the older woman. He closed the door. "Glad to help."

He frowned at Beth. "You've got to find an assistant."

Beth smiled in commiseration. "I did. She starts in two weeks. I think I'll let Lucy go and make it alone for that time."

He nodded. "She was always forgetful, from what I understand, but it's just age that does that. You know, she's probably somewhere in her nineties." He looked thoughtful a moment. "She'd have to be."

"She has a nice way about her and she really tries." A little guilt washed over Beth, talking about the older woman in a negative way.

"She is. She just needs to go home and tend her garden. It's beautiful, by the way. She's still an active person. Just not in this setting. At home, she's right on target. It's just here that she loses her focus. She needs to be where things are familiar."

"I'll visit her when she's at home sometime." After her experiences with Lucy, Beth had a little difficulty believing the woman could survive alone without blowing up her house.

"That's a great idea. She's a hoot and full of tales about the area."

An awkward silence immediately fell on the two. She motioned toward the chair. "Sit down, Dr.

Price. I'm sure you wanted to talk to me or you wouldn't have come."

He sat across from her. "I've been going over my latest figures and stats for the clinic and would like to present a proposal at the next board meeting."

"Your own proposal?" Beth couldn't have been happier. From what she'd seen, the clinic served an overlooked population, the under-insured, of the city and was a needed resource. With Alex's zeal for the project, he'd be the best person to oversee its salvation, if he could find a way to make it pay for itself.

"Yes. I hope you don't mind me asking for the item to be put on the agenda."

"I admit to being a little surprised, but I wish you all the best. I'll see to it you're on the board's agenda in January. Is that suitable? Does it give you enough time?" She jotted down a note to herself to do just that, as well as to do a little more research into the matter herself. It wouldn't do to be unprepared in front of what she suspected was a hostile audience.

"That's great. I appreciate it." He leaned back in his chair noticeably relaxed after having his request granted.

"Dr. Price—"

"Alex." There was that smile again.

She ignored his interruption. "These types of

presentations are really my cup of tea. I would be glad to help you work on it."

"You would? I thought the board didn't want the clinic."

"I'm not speaking for the board, I'm speaking for me. I'd like to help you." Even if her stomach was swimming in acid at the thought of spending any amount of time with him.

"This is amazing. I never dreamed you'd volunteer for this. Thank you. When do we get started?"

"I don't think we should meet here."

"My place is always open," his grin grew wider, but she didn't see any teasing in it.

"No. I don't think we should meet at either apartment." She might be crazy, but not stupid. Not a good idea.

A grin started from one side of his mouth and spread all over his face. "I know just the place. Neutral territory."

"And, that would be where?"

He wrote the address down for her, here in Trentville.

"Fine. We'll get started on Monday evening."

Almost a week later, Beth found herself maneuvering through traffic and down a side street in Trentville with a sense of dread. She'd agreed to meet at Lucy's house, of all places. Alex assured her they'd be able to get a lot done in the evening but she still had her doubts. On her last day of work, Lucy had gotten lost between the bathroom down the hall and her office.

She glanced at the mailbox, 371 Oak Street. That was it. A beautiful Victorian house with royal purple shutters that looked like something out of a fairy tale. The snow on the ground and white icicle Christmas lights only added to the magical quality of the home. The car parked in the drive, a new black sedan, didn't look like a car Lucy Ledbetter would drive, however.

When she opened the door to Beth's knock, Lucy was neatly dressed in slacks and a red sweater, her silver hair a cap of curls. Most surprisingly, she knew exactly who Beth was and warmly greeted her. "Ms. Chambers, you look wonderful. How are things at the hospital?"

Beth shrugged out of her coat and handed it to Lucy. "Things are fine there, Lucy. Thanks for asking. And you're doing well, I hope?"

"Oh, yes. I love being home. Being at the hospital all day leaves me drained. Here I can putter around the house and bake. I love to sew, as well."

Beth followed Lucy as she talked. Aromas of baking brownies and other goodies wafted to her when the kitchen door opened. Alex sat at the table, jotting on a pad of paper, glasses on. He looked up and smiled at Beth but went back immediately to whatever it was he read.

A little disappointed that she hadn't drawn more attention, Beth tried to focus on Lucy's words. "When Alex told me you wanted to work here, I have to admit I was shocked, but I'm so glad you've come. An old girl like me gets lonely. Is there anything I can do?" She glanced at Beth expectantly.

Before Beth could find a way to politely refuse the offer, Alex looked up again with a flirtatious grin. "I hope you know I picked your house due to the snack factor."

Lucy laughed. "Well, young man, if it's coffee and brownies you're after you've come to the right place."

Her phone rang and Lucy ambled to the other room to answer it, throwing over her shoulder for the young people to make themselves at home.

Alone with Alex, Beth was in misery and euphoria at the same time. She realized not seeing him over the past week had been best, because she could now see the affect he had on her. And, she didn't like it. She also didn't like not knowing why she hadn't seen him all week.

However, this was business, all business, and nothing but business, and she intended for it to stay that way.

Then he did something totally unfair. He took off his glasses, grinned lazily, and told her, "I'm sorry

I haven't been around to see you, Beth. Clint Sawyer, in the ER, needed me to cover for him. I've been pulling double shifts."

She grunted. "I didn't expect you to come and see me, Dr. Price."

"I was afraid after last weekend—"

"Don't put any stock in what happened last weekend. Things tend to be different away from the hospital."

He sat back and studied her a long moment. So long in fact, she shifted under the weight of his stare.

"Do you want me to help you with this, or not?" She finally asked.

As if coming back to earth, he shook his head. "Yes. Of course."

"Then let's get at it, shall we?"

"You mean that, don't you?"

"Yes, I don't want to be here all night—" she advanced and placed her briefcase on the table opposite him.

"No, I mean, the part about me and you. You really aren't interested, are you?" His tone was a bit disbelieving.

She'd convinced him. Thank God. "No, I'm sorry but, Dr. Price, you're just not my type."

He replaced his glasses on his face. "I'm sorry. I misread some signals and thought my actions were . . . appropriate."

"Forgiven. Let's just see what we can do to-gether for the clinic." Amazed he'd given up with-out a fight; she told herself she was glad. Glad, confused, and a little saddened, that's what she really was.

"I appreciate that. This clinic is important to the community. We're here for a reason."

"I know you're dedicated, Alex. Now, we have to show the board why. We also need to be able to prove to the board that we can put together a plan so the clinic will at least break even. We don't have to make money, even on a five-year plan. We just have to prove that we won't always be a drain on the hospital's resources." She refused to make eye contact with him as she opened her briefcase and extracted the financial prospectus on the clinic. If he looked too deeply in her eyes he might see the disappointment there.

The swinging door into the kitchen opened, but no one entered. Or so she thought. Suddenly, a small pig wriggled in her lap, licking her on the nose and squealing with delight.

"Joey!" Alex scolded the little guy. "I thought you were in the dining room, eating those leftover donuts that we weren't going to tell your mother about."

He pulled the protesting pig from her lap. With what looked distinctly like a glare at Alex, Joey set-tled down at her feet. "I admit it, Beth, you have an admirer."

"I could do worse." Beth's cheeks flushed. Funny but she wouldn't meet his eyes.

As they worked, Joey licked her knee occasionally, as if to remind her he was there. She'd reach down and scratch his ears or give him something to eat.

The work went smoothly. If nothing else, the clinic had someone on its side that knew accounting and presentations.

Beth amazed Alex.

"I meant to ask you, did you see the new car in the drive?"

"Is that yours?"

"Oh, yeah. Do you know what a car costs nowadays? My payments almost give me a heart attack every time I think about them."

Beth munched a brownie and looked toward the door leading from the kitchen. "Do you think we should check on Lucy?"

Alex checked his watch. An hour had gone by since she took her phone call.

"I suppose so. It wouldn't do much for my reputation if someone died while I was in her home." Alex left the room a moment and returned as Beth grabbed a cookie.

"Still on the phone. She told me to help ourselves to anything we wanted." He grinned that half man–half schoolboy grin that seemed to say so much more than words and asked, "Any ideas, or just settling for coffee?"

She nodded, refusing to join in the joking. "I'll go for the coffee. I thought we'd made it clear that was all I'd be needing."

"Are you kidding? Now that you're really off limits, I plan to tease you mercilessly." If for no other reason, to let off some of the frustration from not being able to be with her. He darted back into the kitchen and returned with a coffee carafe.

"Your sisters must have had it hard growing up." She held her cup up for him to refill.

He poured himself some from the old upright electric percolator. "I guess I played some jokes on them." He ignored her snort and continued, "But you haven't been hazed until baby Tessa does it."

"The pretty blond I met?"

He sat down. "That would be the one. She got mad at me and painted my toenails bright red while I was napping, the day before a big crosscountry meet."

A smile trembled over her lips. "That doesn't seem so bad. A little remover and you're good to go."

"If it hadn't been oil-based house paint, maybe."

She laughed. "That must have been wonderful, to even have someone to raze. I grew up alone. My aunt raised me. We were . . . close." Her eyes held a hurt faraway look.

"I'm sorry. What about your mom and dad?" He stirred a little sugar into his coffee.

"I never knew them."

"That's tough. You know, the little girl with the burns in pediatrics has the same background. Your 'true love' has been doing wonders with her." Joey snorted loud when Alex said 'love.'

"Alex, I have let you get away with some things, but taking a pig to pet therapy isn't going to continue." She frowned.

Alex didn't jump to defend his decision, but made his point gently clear. "Joey is the only one she'll talk to. Darlene or a therapist listens. Joey grunts and rubs his snout against her and she smiles. She hasn't smiled in a year. And the kittens, birds, and dogs haven't done the trick either."

"I suppose I was wrong. I'm sorry. Take him whenever you want."

"Thanks. But, that's everything we're talking about here," he pointed to the paperwork on the table. "It's all we're about. We don't need to care how it happens; we just need to secure safety for people. Whether it's low cost pharmacy, or healthcare, or even charity. We just need to make sure people are cared for, regardless of their financial situation. We can't just say it's good enough. It has to be the best care possible."

Beth could feel something inside her she'd never felt before. It started at the base of her spine and worked its way through her whole body. Without realizing her movements, she leaned forward and kissed Alex long and deep. He pulled her closer into him.

"I can't do this, Alex." She whispered her thoughts and made to pull away. He smoothed a hand along her jaw line, tempting her back to him.

"It'll be okay, you'll see," he returned in a low voice.

"No. It won't. I have to walk down a different path than you do and it can't work."

He stroked her hair. "Why? Why can't we go together down that path, sweetie?"

"This is a conflict of interests." She pulled away. "I have to go. I'll be in touch with you." She grabbed her briefcase, ignoring the sheaf of papers that rested on the table.

"Beth, listen to me."

She ignored him and rapidly walked through the front room and saw Lucy in a chair, still talking on the phone. She muttered a good-bye. "I need to go."

"Coats in the closet by the door, Beth, come again!"

Beth half expected Alex to be hot on her heels, but he wasn't. She grabbed her coat and ran out the door.

She couldn't do this. She just couldn't risk her heart. Not again.

Chapter Five

"**W**ould you please not worry about me?" Beth refolded a pair of jeans and slipped them into Rhoda's suitcase.

"I can't help it. I'm going to be gone until after Christmas. We've spent the holiday together for five years."

"It's okay, honey, really." Beth snuck a small gift-wrapped box into the luggage while her friend's back was turned.

Rhoda brought a sweater to the bed and dropped it on top of the other clothes. "No, it's not. You've been really strange the past few days. I know something's going on you're not talking about. What is it? Is it that doctor?"

"Of course not. Have you thought that maybe I'm really busy and under stress at work?"

"No. That stuff doesn't make you look like you're not feeling well. Have you had a physical exam lately? You're not sick and not telling me, are you?"

"I drink my vinegar, how could I be sick?" Beth managed a smile that she hoped would placate Rhoda for the moment. The woman was too smart for that, with all her flaky attitudes, she was still a great friend and wonderful caring person.

"Just tell me, Beth. Are you okay?" Rhoda straightened and put her hands on Beth's shoulders, staring into her face.

"I am, honey. Really, I am."

"You look so sad."

"The holidays are hard on me. It was the one time Aunt Martha baked and tried so hard to have special things for me."

"Do you want me to go to the cemetery with you?"

"When you get back, we'll go, okay?"

"I don't have to go to my uncle's right now, you know. I can wait until after the first of the year." Rhoda grabbed the sweater she'd tossed in and turned away from the bed. Beth grunted and retrieved the multicolored knit, folding it. She popped it into the case and zipped the suitcase closed.

"Your whole family will be there. I think it would

be wrong for you to miss it. You may never have that chance again. To have everyone together." *Hold it together, Beth*, she thought to herself.

"Won't you come with me?"

"And have you worry about entertaining me instead of enjoying your family? Not on your life." Actually, not going was more for Beth than Rhoda. She'd met the family before.

Rhoda was the most conventional of the whole group.

After more than an hour of the same arguments, Beth hugged Rhoda good-bye and promised they would have their Christmas on New Year's Eve. Rhoda packed her car and drove away.

Beth turned and entered the apartment building alone.

A week before Christmas, and Beth was truly alone.

She bit back tears. She'd do what she always did when she felt sorry for herself. She'd work. She'd work all through the holiday and no one would even have to know she didn't have anyone to spend it with. She'd go in and not even tell anyone she was in the building. She'd work at home and her mind wouldn't be on the fact she was alone and she wouldn't think of Alex Price at all. Not one bit. Not even a little.

With a deep breath, her resolve was strengthened, even if she was lying through her teeth to herself.

*   *   *

Marlene was unimpressed with Alex's dance around the Christmas tree in the empty clinic lobby. "You're no Donny Osmond."

He quit singing "Jingle Bell Rock" and gyrating to his song. "Why would you say such a cruel thing?"

"Because I *like* Donny Osmond."

"You know, somewhere along the line here, we've lost the supervisor slash supervisee relationship. You appear to believe that you can say hurtful things to me and that you expect me not to write you up for insubordination." Like she'd believe that, what with the red hat he wore.

"You don't even know where the forms are. Why would I worry?" She put her coat on and turned out the light in her area.

Alex took the hat off. "All ready for Christmas weekend?"

Alex hadn't had a Christmas off in years. What would he do with himself, he wondered, besides eat until he couldn't move then sleep it off?

They locked up and walked towards the hospital as they talked. "Not as ready as I'll bet you are. This is your first holiday off in how long?"

"Since med school. I can't wait. I'm not even on call. All I have to do is go get Joey from pet therapy and leave. I've even packed for the weekend; I'm staying with my parents. It's going to be great. Cole will be there until after lunch on Christmas day and Tessa and Brian will be there all evening Christmas Eve. Did I mention I'm off duty tomorrow night?"

She chuckled at his obvious good humor. "You did. Dr. Price?"

He quit dancing around her at her quiet tone. "Yes?"

"I hope you have a really Merry Christmas. Thank you for all you do. And the bracelet is beautiful."

The tone of her voice gave Alex notice. "Thank you, Marlene. Thanks for sticking in there. Have a wonderful holiday."

They parted and Marlene headed to her car. Alex went in the side entrance of the hospital and rode up the elevator to the pediatrics wing where he stopped off at the nurse's station. After a couple minutes, he entered an observation room. The therapy room adjacent to it, outfitted with toys, play houses, and colorful beanbags, and a one-way mirror.

In the therapy room, Joey waited patiently at the side of Amber the little girl he'd told Beth about.

Had it only been a week or so? The little blond chattered away to the pig, telling him of her fears, her wish list for Christmas, her belief Santa didn't visit little girls with burn scars in hospitals. Joey grunted and snorted. Obviously, he loved the fact the little girl rubbed his belly the whole time.

Alex joined Darlene by the window and silently watched as a therapist sat on the floor near Amber and Joey. Occasionally, she got a direct response from Amber, but more often she listened as the girl and pig carried on their own conversation.

He really was a great animal for this, Alex saw. By instinct, he knew when to snuffle, when to snort, and when to just snuggle closer to her.

"How's my little guy doing in there?"

"He's amazing. Amber is opening up more than we'd ever hoped. Joey knows just when to respond to her."

"He really can be a good little guy." When he wasn't trying to steal other guys' girls.

Darlene glanced at Alex. "I think you should know I spoke with Beth Chambers."

"What about?"

"She and I talked about the therapy program. She isn't convinced it's a bad thing. You know, Luft doesn't control that woman like we thought he would. She comes up here, almost daily, to see Amber. She's actually very nice."

"I know. She's her own person." Why he should be proud of that, he didn't know, but he was.

Alex waited through the rest of the therapy session and then retrieved Joey. They were on their way out of dodge when he spied Beth approaching the elevator. Joey immediately pulled away from him, pulling the retractable leash to its limit, and darted into the elevator after Beth. Alex followed.

She looked startled for a moment then sent a

smile to the pig, followed by a more reluctant one to Alex. Dang the animal. He was jealous of a pig!

One thing about a pot-bellied pig, or at least this one, he would not be ignored. Joey snorted and sniffed until Beth patted him. Joey then trotted the space of the elevator, pulling Beth with him. It almost forced her to talk to Alex.

Maybe he liked the pig after all.

"So, what does a hospital administrator do on Christmas Eve?"

Beth shrugged tightly. "She works. As she does on Christmas."

No way would he allow that. "You can't do that. Even I'm not working this holiday."

"It's okay, Alex, really." She straightened from patting Joey and faced the doors.

"No, it's not." He took a step toward her.

"Really, it is." She edged away.

"I want you to come to my parents' home."

"Thanks, but no thanks."

"We're going to eat until we're sick and sit around and watch football and Christmas movies."

"As wonderful as that sounds, the answer is still no."

"But, the baby is going to be there," he coaxed.

"No thanks. Really, but no." The elevator stopped and dinged.

He was deflated but not defeated. He knew from experience what it was like to spend Christmas working. "Would you just take my card and call me if you change your mind?"

"Sure." She wouldn't change her mind, but she took the card to appease him.

"In fact, here is my mom and dad's address." He drew the card back and jotted their address and number on it.

"If I change my mind, I'll come." She tried to step around Joey, who'd darted in front of her.

"Or, if you get lonely. You'll come, you promise."

"I promise." She crossed her heart, and made a break for it.

Christmas Eve would be wonderful this year, Beth told herself. She would work until dark, then go home, light up her little Christmas tree, and drink a glass of cinnamon-spiced eggnog. She wouldn't even look on her desk where she had Alex's card with his phone number.

She didn't need a family. She hadn't had one for years, hadn't needed it. But, still, it must be nice to think that she'd have all those people to be around at this season.

Are you out of your mind? Her inner voice screamed at her, *You are hung up on this guy, not his family. What are you thinking?*

Her inner voice had a point. After all, she could hardly keep her hands off the man, much less spend time with him and not imagine herself as being a part of his life.

A part of his life. Those words flew around in her mind. *Could* she be a part of his life?

Could she?

Didn't she want to be part of someone's life?

No, not his. She had to prove she didn't get involved in this work to find a husband. She couldn't get involved. If she got involved it would hurt her ability to stay objective, not to mention her heart.

And, she *would* stay objective.

The clock on the wall chimed ten A.M., the stores were open on Christmas Eve. And they sold small gifts, impersonal gifts, gifts she could give to people if she knew anyone.

If she hit the stores right now, she could find nice little gifts for his family. She could be a part of a family celebration. Not only that, she could spend time with the pig and his uncle.

She thought about the little fellow. He'd be heart-broken without her. She giggled despite herself. What an excuse.

"No." She wouldn't.

Inner voice once again contacted her. *Isn't he worth the risk?*

Beth sprang from her chair and grabbed her coat from the rack near her door. *Wonder what the major pet stores had for pigs?*

Chapter Six

The door opened and Mrs. Price answered it. Beth hoped the first thing she didn't do was show her to the restroom after their first meeting.

She didn't.

"Beth! Alex didn't mention you'd be here tonight! Here, honey, let me help you." The older woman took some of the wrapped presents from her.

"I wasn't sure I'd be able to make it. I didn't have a chance to call him. I didn't want to promise if I couldn't."

Claudette stepped back to let Beth through the door. "Did you have any trouble finding the place?"

"No, none at all." The house was situated on a small hill not far from a main street, but far enough so traffic wasn't overwhelming in front of it. A cute

Donna Wright

Tudor home, all decked out in lights and greenery. It looked wonderful.

The home was modest, but boasted a large fireplace in the den. She took in every picture on the wall, every decoration made from the childhoods of three active children, and new pictures tucked in frames, yet to be strategically placed of the first grandchild.

Alex rounded the corner of the room then came to a full stop. The look on his face, as she removed her coat, was enough Christmas for Beth.

"You made it! You said you weren't sure you would!" He strode purposefully to her and kissed her on the cheek then pulled her into a tight hug. "I can't believe you came," he whispered the words against her hair. His arms around her felt so right.

His mother had somehow disappeared, with all her gifts.

"I don't know how I ended up here. I didn't have any intentions of coming here this morning when I got up." She looked away, afraid he'd see misty eyes.

"But now you're glad you came." His smile was one that told her all she needed to know. He wanted her there. He really did.

"I am." She pulled him close to her and this time she initiated the kiss.

"You know," he told her when they finally came

up for air, his voice husky, "I could get used to you doing that."

"Can we really make this work, Alex?" she didn't meet his gaze but stared at the crew neck of his navy blue sweater.

"Are you kidding?" He released her, took her hand, and led her towards the den, "It's Christmas, everything works at Christmas."

The festivities started with a buffet of finger foods, candles were lit with no television. Not at all like the solitary evenings she had with her aunt. The family talked, laughed, played word games, and drank warm holiday punch.

Joey, though he stayed near Beth, was not above being fed by anyone with an extra tidbit.

Once everyone was stuffed with rich dips and desserts, the television came on.

"This is my favorite holiday tradition," Alex whispered in her ear, tucked her under his arm on the sofa, and pushed play on the VCR remote. The opening credits came on to an old movie. George Bailey stood at a bridge, ready to jump.

By this time, it was almost ten o'clock. She didn't want to leave the warmth of the home. A home filled with love and laughter and all the things that were missing from her upbringing and her life now.

She never wanted to leave. This was what she wanted for her children.

Oh! Children! She shivered at the thought.

"Are you okay, sweetie?" Alex looked down and squeezed her shoulders.

Just be happy. It wasn't her own inner voice she heard, but Rhoda's words echoed through her head. Words she'd heard her friend say a hundred times.

A warmth spilled over her and she turned her face to his with a smile. "I'm great. How about you?"

"Perfect."

"We're not moving too fast, are we?"

"Not at all." His smile returned.

Beth glanced toward her watch. Alex put a hand over her wrist, covering the numerals on the time-piece. Beth glanced up to remind him of the time.

"You don't have to leave, you know. There's plenty of room here. You can have my old room and I'll sleep on the couch."

The words were out of her mouth before she could stop them. "That would be great. Do you have a t-shirt I could sleep in?"

His eyes darkened, "I don't want to think about that, but I still have some old clothes up there. Just get what you need."

"I need a toothbrush," she teased.

"My mom has that room fixed up so a guest will have all that's necessary. Believe me, if you can't find it in there, you don't need it."

Tessa and her husband left, with a promise of returning tomorrow morning with his father and staying until after lunch, after which they would visit other family members.

Danni and her husband retired to their room with the baby.

With Joey at Beth's side, Alex, she, and his parents stayed up talking until the wee hours of the night. Never had Beth felt so welcomed anywhere. She felt as if she'd known the Prices all her life. She especially loved the childhood stories of Alex and the girls and wanted to hear more of some stories that Alex wouldn't allow to be told.

The feeling was incredible.

How could she ever have had a life with no . . . life?

Now, she'd have to return to that lack of sparkle and how could she do that?

Rhoda had been right all along. She needed to settle down and fall in love and have babies.

Claudette Price had had a career. Like her daughter, Tessa, she'd taught school. Danni practiced law. They had it all. She could too.

After Tom and Claudette went to bed, Alex and Beth talked.

"Tell me, Beth. What were Christmases like when you grew up?"

"My aunt and I would stay up on Christmas Eve and watch for Santa Claus, until I learned there wasn't one and then, we'd just stay up because we wanted to. She was a really lovely person."

He stroked the back of her hand with a light finger. "I'm sure she was."

"Then, the next morning, she always had three or four presents for me, mostly clothes. I always had a stocking filled with small toys and lots of fruit and nuts. We'd fix a big breakfast and go to church. After church, we'd come home and fix lunch with chicken, dressing, and pie. I imagine it's nothing like what you do, but it really was a nice time."

"Being with people you care about is always a nice time, Beth. My parents both worked, and we had things, but we had love too. A lot of kids can't say that."

"I know." Her aunt had really loved her; she knew that. Had grown up knowing that, even if she didn't have material things, she had love.

"What about your parents? You never mention them."

"Aunt Martha was my maternal grandmother's sister. Isn't that a mouthful? It appears that no one else in the family, including my parents, wanted to put up with a baby when I was born."

"What became of them?"

"Both have since died." She glanced down at their entwined hands.

"I'm sorry."

They became quiet. Beth let her head fall onto his shoulder and they stared into the fire in silence for a few moments before she had to speak again.

"I like it here, Alex. It's warm and full of fun. But, you know, my aunt, she was a neat lady. You'd have enjoyed being around her, she had a great sense of humor."

"You miss her."

"Yeah, I do. I was lucky to have her."

Alex opened his eyes and found his father sitting in his old recliner beside the sofa, drinking a cup of coffee. "Sorry, son. Didn't mean to wake you."

"Are you kidding?" Alex sat up and pulled his t-shirt down. "I couldn't sleep knowing Beth was here, anyway."

"You really like her, don't you?" His father smiled at him.

"Yeah. What do you think, by the way?"

"Beautiful and intelligent. A lethal combination. All the Price women have it. She'll fit in just fine." His dad smiled and held his cup up in a silent toast.

"Yeah. I'm crazy about her. She's got this real tough woman of the world exterior, but if you get to know her, she's totally different." Alex leaned forward and propped his elbows on his sweatpant-covered knees, clasping his hands together.

"You'll be lucky to hold on to this one, son."

"She's resisting it though Dad."

"Why?"

"I'm not sure. I think she's afraid."

"Afraid? Of what, you?" His father chuckled.

"That'd be like being afraid of the boy next door. Just keep being you and she'll come around. I guarantee."

His mother called from the kitchen, "Who wants breakfast?"

Christmas morning told Alex all he needed to know about Beth. When she saw the presents under the tree in the living room, her green eyes, wide with the wonder of a child's, surprised him.

Her gifts were extremely nice, though he knew she must have bought them at the last minute. His mother opened a sweater; his sisters both had nice perfumes and the men, except Alex, gloves. She'd bought the baby an outfit and a few rattles.

For Joey, Beth bought a sweater. She'd even remembered Danni had a dog, and bought her a big chew bone.

In return, his family had all thought of her and she had several brightly wrapped boxes to open. As a child would, she opened each one and thanked each giver. Then she came to Alex's gift, a silver heart pendant on a sterling chain.

She hugged him tight and thanked him. Then, handed him a box. "I hope this helps you get over your old green bomb." Her smile held mischief.

He couldn't believe when he opened the box, it held a collectible die-cast metal green Nova.

After all gifts had been opened and the group

cleaned up the wrapping paper, Beth caught Alex in the hall and kissed him. "Thanks for the necklace."

"Thanks for being here. You've made my Christmas, Beth."

Alex followed Beth home later that day. The last two days would be remembered, at least in his mind, as spectacular. They got to her apartment and she allowed him to walk her up to her door.

He held her hand. "This is the best Christmas I've had in years."

"I've never had a Christmas like this. Where there was money to buy things and everyone seemed happy. My aunt and I had nothing. A few days after I finished college, she didn't wake up. So, by the time I could have given her things, she was gone. I still have the one thing she left me." She pulled a chain from inside her sweater with a cameo on it.

He touched the antique piece. "It's beautiful."

"No, it's not. It's secondhand. It's cheap. It's . . . all she had on this earth, except me."

"Then, she was a wealthy woman."

"I didn't appreciate her enough."

"Maybe she didn't want material things, Beth. She just wanted your love. And when she died, I'm sure she knew she had that."

"How do you know?"

"Because love teaches love. She taught you how to love and be charitable to others."

They stopped in front of her apartment door.

"I'm not ready to invite you inside. I hope that's all right."

"Not a problem." He didn't bother hiding his disappointment but took it well.

"I had a wonderful time, Alex. I can't believe I had a family at Christmas."

He eyed her solemnly before pulling her into a warm hug. "I'm glad you enjoyed yourself. I'm working a lot between now and New Year's. But, I can get tickets to the big celebration at Ober Gatlinburg if you want to go."

"I don't think so." She shook her head.

His heart fell. "Why not?"

"Rhoda's friend has a party every year that we go to."

"Oh. Okay." He could do that too, if she'd invite him.

"Don't look so down. You can come too." Her smile melted his heart.

"You did that on purpose." He hugged her to him and nuzzled her neck.

"I'm mean that way," she sighed.

"Just another quirk of yours to get used to." He kissed her quick. "I've got to run, but I'll meet you here on New Year's Eve."

"Don't you want to know what time?"

He turned around and walked backward as he spoke, "I'm sure we'll talk before then. Be good."

"You too." She waved.

After she went inside and got settled, she worried. Was she falling for Alex, or was it his family? Did the pig mean as much to her as the home-cooked breakfasts? Did the presents underneath the tree matter more than the man that bought her these things?

She worried as she put her coat and presents away; she gathered her nightgown, turned on the shower, and stood underneath the warm spray.

After her shower, she curled up in the overstuffed armchair and opened a file. She'd stared at the same page for fifteen minutes when the phone rang.

"Hello?"

"Hey. Just wondering if you're thinking about me." His voice warmed her through the wires.

"And if I'm not?"

"Then, you should be."

"Well, in a roundabout way, I am thinking about you. I just picked up the file on the clinic. I think I know someone who can put together a plan or grant without so much paperwork on our end."

"I think I just fell in love with you." His careless words thrilled her, even if they were a joke.

"You say that now, but wait until we're back at work and I'm hounding you about overtime."

"Oops! Better go! Take care!"

"Coward." She laughed.

Chapter Seven

By the next morning, Beth had second thoughts on what she'd done.

One, she'd broken a major rule. Not one of the minor ones, but one that she'd held firm to because of past experience. She'd dated a guy at work and it could lead to nothing but trouble. Just as in her last job, it could mean leaving.

Two, there was a lot of attraction that she hadn't counted on, much more than she felt with Frank Blair. She'd kissed Alex as much as he'd kissed her. He'd let her lead for the first short while, but then, she'd given him signals all was well.

It wasn't.

Oh, God, she'd told him all about her childhood.

He now knew about Aunt Martha, her lean years, even her parents' abandonment.

She'd never shared those things before, not with anyone. Rhoda knew more than anyone else, but before Alex, she'd kept her secrets tight against her. Those were not things she talked openly about, but he had this, this *thing* about him that said, "Tell me all about yourself."

Like an idiot she'd all but slit her wrists and bled her emotions all over.

When she explained all this to Rhoda, Beth was amazed with her answer.

"Okay, Beth. So, you moved a little fast on the personal stuff. So what? If the guy likes you, then why worry?"

"What if he tells these things around the hospital when it doesn't work out?"

"So, now you know the future and you know it won't work out? I think you need to give the guy a break. He's a doctor; he's got this great family. Heck, the guy even has a pig at times. How can you fight that?"

Beth thought a minute while she sipped herbal tea. "That's just it. He's too good to be true. There has to be something about him to dislike."

"Didn't you say he's a jokester?"

"He has a good sense of humor, yes." Beth defended him.

"Would you work with me, here? I'm trying to find something minor wrong with the guy so you won't let him get away."

"I've got it. I'll go through his files tomorrow. I'll check everything about the clinic and the good doctor and then I'll be able to make a better, more informed decision, less affected by all the holiday hoo haa."

"This is a man, not a stock to buy or sell," Rhoda huffed.

"After tomorrow, I'll know what kind of man I'm dealing with."

Rhoda rolled her eyes. "Good grief."

Monday was a strange day for Alex. He'd worked all night Sunday to give an ER doctor some time off with his family and then went straight into work that morning.

He wasn't as used to this schedule as he'd once been. When he'd interned, this workload meant nothing. But, not now. *I'm getting soft.*

And, speaking of soft, he pulled his cell phone from his lab coat pocket as he crossed the street to the clinic. He needed to hear one soft, smooth voice and he knew just where he'd find her, too.

She answered her private office line.

"Good morning. Have a nice weekend?"

A long pause made Alex wonder if she'd heard him.

"How do you have this number?" Was he imagining it or had her tone changed from the warm soft tones to a crisp, cool tone?

He smiled. "Have you forgotten to whom you speak? I am Alexander Price, the man with all the secrets of the hospital locked up in my brain. I know it all."

Another pause gave him a strange feeling. "Beth, are you okay?"

He heard her try to recover. "Sure. I'm fine. You just caught me in the middle of something."

He paused halfway across the street and a car honked at him. "Sorry!" He yelled, then returned to her. "You sound as if you don't even know me."

"I don't mean to, I'm just in the middle of something."

He sighed. Something wasn't right here. "I can meet you at Lucy's tomorrow night."

"Lucy's?"

"Do you remember the clinic paperwork?" The stuff she kept reminding him to get done.

"Oh, yeah. We need to put some figures together. A friend of mine can write some of our grants for us."

"That's great. Less work on us with the same result. How are things on the front?"

"The front?"

"You know, Luft." Alex opened the door to the clinic and strode into his office.

"I haven't heard from him. Did you expect me to?"

"I've heard that after the first of the year, Luft will hit three things. One will be the clinic."

"Two will be pet therapy," she added.

"You catch on quick, oh beautiful one."

"What's three?"

"Haven't heard. Let me know if you find out anything."

"I really need to go Alex, I'm—"

"Yeah, I know, in the middle of something. Tomorrow night?"

"Seven o'clock?"

"Pick you up then."

He snapped his cell phone shut. This wasn't good. He didn't know what wasn't good. All he knew was she acted so strange on the phone. So, what should he do now? His little voice inside began a tirade about her. She sent mixed signals and had no idea what she wanted. All of it he admitted was true. But he also had to ask himself, why?

After Beth went through Alex's personnel file with a fine toothcomb, she came to one decision. There was nothing wrong with the man that should give her concern.

That concerned her. He couldn't be perfect. She recognized the fact that she'd moved too fast, he worked for her, and fear rolled in her stomach at the mere thought of another involvement.

Tuesday arrived and despite Beth's misgivings she'd have to meet Alex again to discuss clinic business. Lucy decided to go to her daughter's house, so it was just the two of them. The very reason that they'd chosen Lucy's was they looked for neutral territory. Now there was nothing neutral about it. They were alone.

Beth had left him a message that she didn't need to be picked up. She didn't take her coat off before she entered the dining area. Alex munched some brownies Lucy had left and looked at her when she arrived. She didn't get the smile she expected.

"You want to tell me what's going on, Beth?"

"I've decided not to go to the party on Friday night." She perched on the edge of her seat, still in her coat.

"I'm not surprised. You've done a one-eighty, so can I at least ask why?"

"I moved too fast, Alex. I know I shouldn't have, but I did. I know you're not happy, but I can't do this."

He answered with an impersonal nod.

"We've done a lot of work and I think we can get grants and other funding both through and without the hospital."

His voice chilly, he thanked her for what she'd done. "I appreciate your work on this. In just a couple of weeks you've done what I never thought of doing."

"Your job isn't, and shouldn't be, finding money for the clinic."

"What about us, Beth?" he pressed.

"I can't do that. We work together, more clearly, you work for me. Doesn't that just sound wrong to you?"

"No, it sounds like a cop-out. I'm man enough that your position at work means nothing to me. I'm not afraid of falling for the boss. In fact, I have."

"Christmas is a time when everything seems magical. Especially for someone like me who never really knew a family Christmas."

He stood. "So, you were all magical feeling and now I get to . . . what?"

"I don't know how I can thank you for getting me through the holiday," she hedged.

"Take your coat off and sit down. We can talk about what's really bothering you—"

"No." She checked her watch. "I have to go. I have a meeting with the finance committee, believe it or not."

"I don't."

"Are you calling me a liar?"

He stood to face her off, his face set in, for once, hard lines. "No, I'm calling you a coward. Why can't you just let me in, sweetie? I won't hurt you."

"There are no guarantees."

"Life doesn't come with them."

"Well, I need them. I'm leaving."

"Leaving?"

"It doesn't mean that I'm abandoning the clinic."

"No, you're just getting away from me."

"I'll see you at work." She backed away from him.

"If that's how you want it, Beth, fine. But, you need to know that I'm not leaving the door open. You're not going to bounce me around like a tennis ball."

She turned and left.

"And, in tennis love means nothing." Alex threw his pencil down on the table.

Chapter Eight

"Where's your date?" Rhoda put on her shawl. The outfit she wore was so . . . her. A broomstick skirt and sweater. Her jewelry, antique and large, didn't match the multi-colored skirt or sweater, but somehow it fit.

Beth slipped her coat on. "He couldn't make it."

"Oh. Did Dr. Alex have to work?"

"Yes. Yes, he's working." *He did take the ER tonight*, she thought, *so I'm not lying.* After they had their conversation, he volunteered. Being the administrator gave her privy to all hospital information.

Come Monday morning, things would be better. She'd be back at work, herself and all would be well. And tonight she'd go to the New Year's Eve party and have a good time.

The party was a total waste of time, as soon as it was over she and Rhoda went home and straight to bed.

The new year found her in the office; because there was a complete lack of anything else to do and she was so fidgety she couldn't stand herself.

The work paid off. She was summoned to a called board meeting on Monday. Most of the board was there, despite the holiday weekend, more than the quorum needed to make a decision. Which made her wary. The fact Darlene Thompson and Alex were both there added to her suspicions.

Darlene and Alex stood to the side of the door of the conference room, talking quietly. When Beth approached, it was Darlene who took the step towards her. "What's happening, Ms. Chambers?"

"I don't know."

"You expect me to believe that? You are the administrator, you know what's happening all over this hospital at all times. I've seen it more than once." Darlene crossed her arms across her chest and glared at Beth.

"I don't know, Dr. Thompson. Really."

"We're ready." Gordon Luft grinned at them. "I think you're all going to be excited at the changes we're making. We wanted to make sure we'd be able to vote and know the outcome immediately."

Beth's stomach turned over. Something had to be going on that would involve the three of them. In light of Luft's apparent happiness it couldn't be good. The truth was he didn't like any one of the three of them. Beth being a woman was enough for him, but between the pet therapy and the clinic, Alex and Darlene were in the death seat as well.

Luft opened the meeting; the secretary's report and treasurer's report were both waived. Another bad sign.

"Let us get to the reason we're here. First, we'll look at the hospital. As we all know, there are a few departments that don't pull their weight. The urgent care clinic and the pet therapy department."

"I agree." Another board member echoed Luft's words.

"I don't," yet a third member disagreed. "We are a responsible group of people who, at one time, put these things in operation for a reason."

"I have some figures in front of me, thanks to our new administrator, that reflect both items are, at this time, a drain on valuable hospital resources," Luft argued.

Alex looked away from Beth at that moment. The folder that Luft held was from Lucy's. The same file that held the figures for the clinic they had used for their proposal. The last time she'd seen it had been at Lucy's house. She'd left it there, totally by accident.

"Where did you get that?" Beth interrupted.

"Please, you're not a board member, Ms.

“You stole that, didn’t you?”

“I’ll have to ask you to leave if you can’t behave yourself, Ms. Chambers.” Luft’s face began to flush with anger.

“Do I hear a motion that we close the pet therapy department and the urgent care clinic?” He totally snowballed the meeting.

The motion was made and, though not unanimous, was carried.

“How long do we have?” Alex broke his silence.

“Three months. You both have three months to clear up any unfinished business. Unfortunately, there won’t be any openings for either of you here, when that business is complete.”

“This board owes Ms. Chambers a debt of gratitude. In less than thirty days, she’s already recovering money from the budget that we could only have dreamed of a year ago. If there’s no other business, this meeting is adjourned.”

Darlene turned to her, “Thanks a lot. You witch. All the time acting as if you were trying to save my job, caring about the kids I work with. And now where am I?” She shoved past Beth.

“Alex,” Beth turned to him, “I knew nothing about this.”

“Oh, I know that. You are totally innocent of this whole incident.” His words may have been conciliatory but the tone of his voice negated any good feelings.

The room emptied as they talked, many of the board members avoiding them.

"You are a piece of work. You got under my skin and used that to your advantage. All that's important to you is that almighty bottom line. You knew when you opened up to me about your past, I understood you."

He stood close to her, his voice quiet so they didn't attract attention from anyone. But where his voice had held warmth before, now Beth shivered from the chill. "I could see why you'd be that way. But, here's a big surprise that I really didn't expect, while I'm so over my head for you the past few weeks, you're stabbing me in the back, and I'm too love sick to even catch on. You are good. Very good."

"Do you really believe that?"

"Oh, yeah. I do. That's why you've been so distant. You knew what you were doing and couldn't face me."

"No, Alex. Look, it can't work between us, but—"

"Just don't. As if I'd have anything to do with you after all you've done. Go your way, Ms. Chambers. Leave us working class people to our jobs." He started to turn from her then pivoted to face her again.

"Oh, no! Excuse me, I mean to find new jobs. You'd better remember that my sister is an attorney and I expect the severance package made in heaven. And, remember that for Darlene as well. I'll fix you. Just wait."

He stormed out without giving her a chance to respond. All that remained were Beth and Gordon Luft. Luft remained in his chair and leaned back to fold his hands over his belly.

"Problems, Ms. Chambers? Maybe you should give your notice and find a job where you're more appreciated."

Beth swung around to face him. "You obstinate, lying, horrible man. How could you do such a thing? Don't you know what you're dealing with in Alex Price?"

"He's a fool. That's all he'll ever be. I don't worry about men like him."

"Well, you should. Alex Price's sister is an attorney. Did you forget that? And *he's* not a lightweight, no matter how easy-going he appears to be."

"I have kept everything legal. I won't put myself, or the hospital at risk."

"You are out of your mind. And, to pull me into this. Why? What was your reasoning?"

"Lucy and I had a long talk. It seems she was unaware that you were acting without hospital authorization on the clinic project." He used quotes with his fingers.

"I'm the administrator and I decided to help one of the departments make money. You should be jumping up and down."

"When I heard about your little project, I went to talk to Lucy. She was appalled to be involved and gave me all the information you left there."

She shook her head. To take advantage of the old woman was just another indication that Luft was a sleaze of the third degree.

"I really don't think you should stay here. After this, there are no employees that will feel like they can, or should, trust you. It would be better for all involved, when you really think about it."

Beth fumed. "No, as I really think about it, I don't think so. I do think, however, that you and I will be at odds for a while. That is, if *you're* still here."

Beth left before he could say more.

What a way to start the week.

Alex and Darlene had lunch, what they could get down, at the cafeteria. The news spread like wildfire through the hospital that they were on notice and people treated them as if they had something contagious.

"I'd have thought people would want to sympathize." Darlene took a bite of potatoes.

"They're just job scared. It's how it works. When someone is put on notice, everyone knows it could be him or her next. It's easier just to ignore us. And we should do the same."

Darlene's staff worked on the pediatrics wing, so they were safe, but Alex suddenly realized, he hadn't let Marlene know.

He excused himself and hurried to the clinic. He found his assistant crying. "I knew this day would come, Dr. Price. I knew it. I just didn't really believe it. That doesn't make sense, does it?"

He put his arms around her in a brotherly hug. "It makes all the sense in the world. I wish I could promise you something else, but I'm on notice as well."

"I know that. I feel even worse for you, because this was your dream. At least for me, I can find another job, but where will you get another dream?"

He released her and she grabbed a tissue. "And, what did Ms. Chambers do about this?"

"She," he couldn't tell the truth, "didn't do anything."

"She's the administrator! Didn't she try to help you at all? I thought you two, you know."

He hated the truth, but he told her anyway. "Ms. Chambers gave the board the information it needed to do what it did."

"That's not possible. She wouldn't do that."

"Your sources had started to think she was okay. She's not."

"You've lost your job, your dream, and your heart is broken."

"No, it's not. I'm just facing the truth. I'm glad I found out before anything happened."

"I thought you spent the holidays with her." She dabbed at her eyes.

"How in the world did you know that? Don't tell me. Your sources. Sheesh."

After Marlene calmed down, they both tried to have a normal day. The difficulty on that meter strained even more, when signs were sent over to put in the lobby regarding the closing of the clinic.

Always the first one with a joke, always the happy one, Alex surprised himself when at the end of the day, he got in his car, slammed the door a few times, and hurled expletives at his steering wheel.

It wasn't the clinic. Not all of it. In fact, he knew that the clinic was and would always be on thin ice. No. It was what she had done. How could he have trusted her at all? How could she have pretended to be saving the clinic when all along her goal had been to get enough information to close not only the clinic but the pet therapy as well?

The witch. The auburn-haired green-eyed witch.

He had an idea. He started the car in jerky motions. "I'll show you, lady, just what Alex Price is made of."

* * *

Beth went to her office in a stupor. This couldn't be happening to her. But it was. Luft was not the idiot she'd thought him to be. Oh, no. He was not only smart, he was callous and that was a lethal combination.

Darlene Thompson wouldn't see her and Beth had no intention of trying to reach Alex at this point.

She'd never seen anyone so angry. Never. She sat down at her desk, locked the office door and cried. "Dear God, what have I done?"

She put the pieces together in her head. They met at Lucy's and somehow, Luft had gotten the file from her. But, how?

Okay, that's point one. Get to Lucy and ask how this all took place with Luft, Beth planned.

Second, her actions, her distance, and her damnable obstinacy that kept her from opening up to Alex was what caused him to think she was guilty. How could he not?

And, Luft. He thought that she'd resign now that she and Alex had separated. That rat. No, that would be giving rats a bad name.

She pulled herself together and went up to the pediatric wing. Joey the pig found her immediately. "You're all I've got left. I better be good to you," she patted his head and scratched under his chin.

Dr. Thompson totally ignored her. Not only that,

except for speaking when they were spoken to, all employees stayed a distance.

This could be worse, but she wasn't sure how.

At home that evening, Rhoda listened as Beth explained everything that happened. She couldn't believe the audacity of Mr. Luft.

"So, what's the plan?" Rhoda asked as she tried to drink her vinegar concoction.

Beth, too, to please her friend had some in her drink. She finally told Rhoda, "I have it all worked out."

"Anything I can do to help?"

"First, don't ever give me the vinegar stuff again." She put her cup down on a coaster. "Second, pray that the people I need to work with on my plans will be receptive to doing lots of things they wouldn't normally do."

Chapter Nine

"So, she broke your heart and took your clinic too?" Hugh Cramer reached for the box of lo mien from across the table.

Alex smirked. "All this kind sympathy from a friend is too much, Hugh. Just way over the top. Even for you."

"Let me tell you something, old pal. The clinic has no legs to stand on."

"But, private information regarding clinic business was given to Luft to use against it, Hugh. Doesn't that account for anything? These were things he wasn't aware of until Beth gave him the file."

"What can be private from a board member, Alex? You know better than this, you're no idiot.

What's the real problem? Or is it a legal one?" Hugh eyed him sagely.

Alex leaned back in his chair. "Listen, I want to know something and I didn't want to ask Danni."

"Now we're getting somewhere. I only hear from you Prices when you're keeping secrets."

"Beth tricked me into trusting her. She pretended . . ." his voice trailed.

"Pretended? Oh, *pretended*. So, you're asking me is there anything illegal in the way she got her information for the board? No. Because the information wasn't illegal to begin with."

"So, there is no recourse for me to take. Great." Alex dropped his chopsticks into the box of fried rice.

"No legal recourse, no. But, you appear to be mad enough to spit. So, tell me, did this woman take advantage of you?"

Alex groaned. "You could say that. She spent the holidays at my parents' house. She gave me a certain amount of affection. Truth is I feel like some kind of idiot. Hugh, how in the world did I get taken in?"

"Is that a rhetorical question?"

"Do you have an answer if it's not?"

It was Hugh's turn to lean back. "I think so. You see your family all settled and you want that too. Pretty girl comes along, at least from the way you're acting I assume she's pretty—"

"Beautiful, really."

"My point made, and you think, why not me?"

"Yeah." Alex looked away. "Why not me?"

"You know, old pal, I can't help you with this one."

"I know."

"Then, why did you invite me over?"

"Because you said you'd buy. Anyway, I thought we'd play a game of pool before you left." The graduation gift from his family got little use.

"Oh, no. Do you really think I'm in the mood to hang out with some broken-hearted pathetic guy?"

"I'd kind of hoped, yeah."

"Well, twenty bucks a game, then."

"I'm about to be unemployed."

"Fine. Fifteen."

Alex pushed back from the table. "Five and not a penny more."

"If you thought you had a chance of winning, you'd bet more so you'd have retirement."

Lucy answered her door and recognized Beth right away. She looked not only shocked but a little frightened when she saw her. "Beth, dear, why are you here?"

"I need to talk to you, Lucy. May I come in?" Beth kept her voice level and soft so she didn't intimidate the woman.

Lucy looked past Beth and around the neighbor-hood as if she expected to see someone else there. Alex, perhaps? "I suppose it would be alright." She stepped back to let Beth in.

"Aren't you well?" Beth worried from the way the older woman acted.

"I must be honest with you, Beth. Mr. Luft appeared upset with me for allowing you and Alex to come here."

"Why do you think that was, Lucy?"

"He said you two were plotting against him, Beth. I wanted to know your side of the story, but was afraid to call the hospital." Lucy led her into the living room.

"May I sit down?"

"I'd rather hear your story before we go through the actions of being courteous."

"I wanted to save the urgent care clinic. That's all. It had nothing to do with Mr. Luft. Except he wanted to close it. I was not plotting against him, as a person, I just wanted to help Alex save not only his job, but the community service of the clinic. Now Alex thinks I gave the file to Luft that showed our work. The clinic will close. The pet therapy department is closing as well. I've been put in a sit-uation where everything I've tried to do was right but has been misconstrued. I need your help." Beth kept the tears out of her voice with effort.

"My word! What can I do?" Lucy led her to a

sofa and gestured for her to sit before grabbing both hands.

"Can you remember what day Mr. Luft came by and got the file?"

"Oh, yes. I remember, because my daughter was here as well. We had tea. Iced tea, even though it was cold as Moses' knickers outside. It was the day after Christmas. Someone told him you two had met here. He wanted to ask me why. My Linda told him I could have whomever I wanted as a guest, but he said that the two of you plotted against him and he needed all the information I could give him, so I gave him the file. Should I call Alex and tell him what happened?"

Beth pondered that a long moment. "No. It would just look as if I had you do that."

"Then what should I do, dear? I'd like to help you."

"I'll let you know. Thanks for telling me the truth." She gave the woman a swift hug to indicate no hard feelings. All in all, Lucy was just another of Luft's victims.

Beth left and went back to the hospital. The calls she'd made that morning had been returned. She'd go to Louisville tomorrow. Joseph Lane could definitely help her in this situation.

After a sleepless night she pulled out of her parking lot. She had to accomplish three things on this trip. She had to save the pet therapy department. She had to save the clinic. And, with the situation at hand, she had to find a job.

It had been true all along. Luft, the jerk, hired her only because she'd fallen and he was afraid she'd sue. This had been a good deal. Get rid of Alex, the clinic, the "zoo," and her all in one fell swoop. In the aftermath, there would be no team against Luft, either, because everyone was so angry at her, she wouldn't have the influence to help them. As much as she liked Darlene and Alex, they were doctors, not business people. Luft knew that too.

She hoped that he could sleep nights.

What a lie. She hoped that his sins kept him awake for months and he never had another decent night's sleep. She didn't think she ever would.

She knew she'd never have another wonderful, family Christmas.

But, she couldn't blame Luft for that, and maybe that was a part of what made her so mad at this situation. She wanted to blame the man for everything, but her insecurities had played right into his hands.

She cursed the road, the driver in the car next to her, and then herself.

Aunt Martha would have washed her mouth out with soap.

*   *   *

"That's Gene Hackman." He tipped the soft drink bottle up high to get the last drop. "Yep, that commercial is Gene Hackman. And, the one before that, *that* was definitely Keifer Sutherland. You know what's really sad, not only am I talking to myself, alone in my home, but I'm watching TV and listening to commercials to the point that I can tell you who the voice is doing the narration." Alex glanced around the room. He didn't even have Joey here as an excuse.

Sad.

The phone rang. "Your dime."

"It's more like fifty cents, isn't it?"

"Hey, Darlene. What's going on?" Alex eyed his sock-covered feet, crossed and propped on the crate that served as his coffee table. His socks were getting thin in the toes, but he'd not be able to buy another pair for a while.

"I need that pig of yours."

"You need Joey? I thought Danni left him there."

"Mike picked him up last night and Amber had a terrible nightmare about the fire. Now she wants to see Joey and I can't reach them. You have a number?"

"Yeah. I always forget her cell number, let me look it up for you." He walked to the kitchen and put the phone back to his ear. "So, any news from the hospital sources to tell me about?"

"I heard that Luft and Beth had a big fight. She

isn't supposed to be in for the next few days. I don't know why."

"So is she out of town?" Why'd he care?

"Yeah. That new assistant of hers doesn't know why. She's looking for a job, too. She's not sure if Luft will keep Beth on now that she got rid of us."

"That doesn't make sense to me no matter how I cut it. Oh, here's Danni's cell number."

"You know, Alex, something isn't right about this whole thing. She decides she's going to help us, then gives info to Luft. Then, stands there while he ruins her with us."

"Here's the number." He tried not to concentrate on what she said as he gave it to her.

After she wrote it down, she asked him again what he thought.

"Darlene, I'm just going to be honest. I'm trying not to think about her at all right now. She betrayed me in every way."

"I'd heard you two were dating."

"How did you hear that? How does this hospital get all the information on everything?"

"The hospital grapevine is known all over the world as the most reliable source of communication. The lines never go down. Neither rain, nor sleet, nor anything else that can stop even the postman, can stop the hospital grapevine."

"It can, however, get its wires crossed."

"So, you guys weren't dating," Darlene pressed.

"Yes. But, that's not what's important."

"In this case, sure it is. You're hurt and you're a man. That means to stay manly you can't talk about it. You won't either. You'll suffer. Not my fault."

"You know, Darlene. After you get hold of Danni, maybe we could get something to eat."

"Oh, you want to talk?"

"I think so." Maybe he needed to air this with someone who knew Beth, who could give him some hope.

Chapter Ten

Beth's emotional exhaustion outweighed her physical fatigue by tons. No one could be that stupid, she told herself again and again, no one.

Yet, she ached. Not from the journey from Louisville. Not from meeting and re-meeting and meeting again to rehash the same thing.

She longed for family and the man that could give her just that. She loved Alex. She knew that now. She wiped scalding tears away from cheeks chapped from the weeping.

She knew now that all she'd had to do was let Alex in. The question was could she ever let anyone in?

She wasn't sure, even now.

Her trip was a new start for her, she reasoned.

She wouldn't leave the hospital in a mess. She knew what that type of administrator was like. She'd been left, as an assistant, to clean up after one in the past and she wouldn't do that to anyone, if she could help it.

She wondered what Darlene, and of course, Alex must think. She couldn't believe that aside from the fact she needed a job, the clinic would close, the pet therapy shut down, and in the end she was to blame.

She knew she'd done nothing to attain that status.

Luft, however, didn't know her. He'd done no research on her whatsoever. She'd see to it he'd pay for underestimating her.

After pulling into the parking lot of her apartment, she unpacked the car and hauled her bags upstairs. The Louisville trip had lasted several days, yet she was surprised at how much she'd accomplished.

If the weekend brought what she thought it might, Luft may just have some things to deal with that he didn't expect. The thought, even though her heart still ached, made her smile.

She couldn't blame Luft for everything. Some of it was her own fault, but she could certainly take her anger out on him.

Things were in order when she opened her apartment door. All was quiet and orderly; as she'd left them, with only phone messages to indicate she'd been gone.

She pressed the recall button with a desperate hope. Several of the messages were from Rhoda. She'd hoped Beth had called in and gotten them because she'd lost her cell phone number. She dialed Rhoda to reassure her she was home safe and sound.

"I, um, need to tell you something." Rhoda sounded a bit unsure.

"What?"

"When I got home from work yesterday Alex was here, waiting for me."

"Was he looking for me?" Beth held her breath.

"Kind of. I told him you were still gone and he asked all kind of questions."

"About what?"

"About you, your family, the job, and whether you'd seemed happy in the job. If you said anything about the clinic or pet therapy."

Beth was silent and her friend took it as a sign to continue. "I told him the only thing you ever mentioned was the good work both programs did and that the pig was the star of the pet therapy program."

Beth thanked Rhoda and again guaranteed her she was fine. She rung off and checked the rest of her messages.

The next message cheered her. She'd gotten a job in Louisville. Once again the tears started to flow. She hated to leave here, leave her friend and apartment. But, she knew after Alex, she would need to get out of the area.

She couldn't stay here knowing he was so close.

"A new start on life." The words, when spoken aloud, gave her little comfort. "I can do this. I can have it all, and I will."

She readied for bed with a heavy heart and her mind racing toward the goals she'd set and those she'd already met. Suddenly the material goals didn't seem as alluring as before.

Alex turned the alarm clock off and sat up in bed. He couldn't sleep and there was no reason to lie there staring at the ceiling.

His job was history and he didn't know if the clinic could be bought by another entity. If it could, with it being a money drain who would want it?

He loved the work he did in the clinic; it was what he felt he was meant to do. But he didn't know how well he would do being unemployed.

He and Darlene had talked about going into private practice, but good Lord; the paper work would kill a goat and neither of them were that good at it. If they had a private practice, there'd have to be a wunderkind clerk out there to save them from bankruptcy.

He went to the fridge and got the milk out then tilted the carton to drink. His mother's "tsk, tsk, tsk," rang through his mind. "It's my milk, Mom. No one else drinks from it."

He sighed. No jade-eyed beauty with luscious auburn curls.

He slammed his fist on the kitchen table. The table jarred and bumped into the kitchen wall it rested against, knocking the wall clock from its anchor. Alex cursed lividly as he sidestepped around the now shattered clock.

Life, if nothing else, was not fair. The words echoed in his mind.

The witch in beautiful lady's clothing ruined not only his life, but an entire community who stood to suffer because he'd let his guard down.

He quit being the reliable but funny Dr. Alex. Now he was the unemployed and not-so-funny Dr. Alex. He needed to get moving, instead of feeling sorry for himself. He glanced toward the wall. No clock.

He picked up the phone and dialed.

A woman's voice answered, sounding almost human in the recording. "Thank you for calling the National Bank. Don't you need a loan today? If so, we can help! Give us a call! The time is four seventeen A.M., the temperature is thirty-seven degrees."

He went into the bathroom and grabbed his shaving cream. He may as well get some breakfast; there would be no sleep.

After he cut himself three times, he managed to get shaved, get dressed, and get downstairs to his car. His new car wasn't so great. He didn't like the fact it started with no problems. He wanted to go back to his old car with the places where his rear fit into the leather, the torn leather of the front seat.

He missed his car, she'd seen him through too much to abandon. He was in that car when he got the call he'd passed his boards.

He'd studied in that car when the dorm was so noisy he couldn't hear himself think.

Bottom line, that car was a part of him and now it was in some junkyard in Kentucky.

He pulled his car into a parking slot and glanced up through the windshield. Great, without knowing it, he'd driven to Beth's apartment. Maybe he could start a new career, Stalkers Are Us.

Her light was on.

He checked his watch. Five A.M. and her light was on.

He wasn't the only one not sleeping. Good.

If her conscience forced her to stay awake, it served her right.

A shadow crossed the curtain then again, and again. She was awake and she was pacing.

After battling his own conscience, his ego, and his sense of self-preservation he turned the engine off, exited the car, and quickly strode to her apartment door.

He knocked softly as to not wake the neighbors.

She didn't answer.

"Beth. It's me." He called through the door.

She opened it, looking as if she'd been through a storm and back again. Her eyes were red and he asked himself if she'd been crying.

"What are you doing here?"

"May I come in?"

She backed up, allowing him entrance. Empty boxes lay around the apartment.

He faced her as she closed the door.

"This is my home, Alex, at least for a while. So if you have something to say, all I ask is that you do it quietly."

He opened his mouth to ask her why she screwed the clinic, but instead he asked, "I thought we were friends. In fact, I thought we were more than that."

She ignored the personal comment and instead talked about the hospital. "I've been working on the clinic and pet therapy program. I can't go into a lot of detail right now. I hope to help you, if I can."

He couldn't take a chance on believing her. "To help me? After giving us up to Luft? You amaze me."

"I didn't give you up."

"If not you, then how did he get the file?"

"Lucy." She gestured toward a chair.

"What? Lucy? You're going to lay the blame on a little old lady who was willing to let us use her home?" He flopped down on her sofa not believing for a moment what she said.

"Luft caught wind that we met there and went to

visit her. He convinced her we were plotting against him. I think he made her think she would be banned at the hospital."

All the wind left his sails. "He went to her house and threatened her? Lucy? That sweet white-haired lady gave him the file because she was scared." He shook his head. "Not even Luft could sink that low."

She bristled. "No, but I could, is that it? You'd rather believe me to be some type of monster than to call Luft on what he did. It's easier that way, isn't it?"

"What would you have me think? At least I didn't go hot then cold so I could sabotage the clinic. I put it together that all of it was to get to the clinic."

"I won't dignify your idiotic judgments with an answer."

"Didn't you get the point the other day? The clinic is closing. The doors are being shut and we're being booted. That's Darlene and I. You're well set."

"No, I'm not. I'll get the brunt of this from the community and will be replaced for coming up with this debacle. As you said once before, Luft comes out smelling like a rose and I come out the bad guy."

"So, what happens?"

"I'm in the process of some business that will be best for all concerned."

"Are you going to share this brilliant plan?"

"No. I see no reason to tell you anything at this point. It'll be easier to just do the job and leave quietly."

"And, us?"

"There is no *us*." She stood from where she'd sat on a chair opposite him.

"Okay. Then I guess I may as well go."

"I think that's best."

"You have it all worked out."

"I've been doing some traveling. One has a lot of time to think."

He nodded. "When will I see you again?"

He didn't need all the information she possessed at this time. "At work. When necessary."

"Fine. I'll see you around."

She smiled and nodded as he opened the door and left. "No you won't." He was gone before the words were out of her mouth. But, that was okay. They weren't really intended for him, anyway.

The office door was locked and when she tried her key it surprised her that it opened. She wouldn't have put it past Luft to change her lock. She sensed more trouble ahead since he hadn't. Unease permeated the air of the entire hospital. She checked her schedule on the computer. A few buttons pressed and she learned it had been accessed while she was away, but not changed.

Her email had been accessed as well, but that was her hospital email, not her personal box. If Luft saw what she had under her hat, he'd fall dead of a heart attack.

She paused and giggled. Maybe she should run upstairs to his office and tell him everything. She shook her head. No, of course she wouldn't. She didn't want him dead, just off Alex's back. But at least she was keeping her sense of humor. Or had Alex's rubbed off on her?

A sound from her computer startled her, though it was soft. "What's this?" She asked the monitor.

An email from Luft's secretary announcing a called board meeting. As administrator, she was on the mailing list and evidently Luft hadn't thought to remove her name. She'd returned just in time. According to the attached agenda, the purpose of the business meeting was to discuss her dismissal.

This is going to be so good. She heard her aunt's words in her ears, "Revenge is not sweet, little girl."

"Actually, Aunt Martha, it's best when served warm."

Chapter Eleven

The board gathered right on time, as always, and waited for Luft to start. As the chairman, he sat at the head of the long table and appeared extremely surprised to see Alex sitting near the wall.

Alex suspected the older man thought he'd just wait for his layoff slip.

He smiled to himself. Alex would do all he could, and he could do more than Luft gave him credit for. The biggest mistake people made about Alex was underestimating him. The impression he gave, and he was well aware of it, was he was just a guy out for fun.

He let people think that, in fact, he wanted people to think that. When it came time to go to the mattresses or put on the gloves, or however one wanted to say it, that's when Alex's demeanor played well for him.

Like it would tonight.

He looked to his left and smiled at Sara Smith. She had a new engagement ring on her finger, and no stars in her eyes where Alex was concerned. But, what she *did* have was a camera. Sara worked for the *Trentville Daily Times* and Alex let his friend know right off that she was there to make it hard on Luft. Hard on anyone who wanted to close the clinic.

"We'll come to order in just a moment." He looked at Alex. "You and your friend there will have to leave, this is a closed meeting."

"Oh, I'm sorry Mr. Luft, but according to my sister, you know the one who owns that pig, there is something called a Sunshine Law in the State of Tennessee. That means—"

"I know what it means, Dr. Price." Could the man be more irritated?

"For everyone's sake I'll still explain. It means that anyone in the community can attend these meetings, since this is a community-based hospital."

"We'll be talking personnel policies here, Dr. Price. Your Ms. Chambers will be the subject of our discussion. Are you sure you want the *Times* to hear this?"

He stood. "Let me introduce you to my friend, Sara. She writes for the *Times* and wanted to ask you some questions. As for *Ms.* Chambers, she doesn't belong to me, Mr. Luft. I also find it strange she wasn't invited here for her own lynching."

"But I'm here, all the same." Beth entered the room and advanced to the long conference table. She ignored Alex's gaze but met Luft's surprised one as she placed her briefcase on the table.

Alex grinned. Good girl. Stick up for yourself.

"The meeting hasn't been called to order, Ms. Chambers. I'm sure Mr. Luft will want you here before he hangs you out to dry. Then again, I'm not sure that there'll be a meeting tonight."

Murmurs from the other board members filled the air.

Luft looked around the table in an effort to take back control. "Of course there is. I called a meeting. There will *be* a meeting."

"Mr. Luft, I know you think me some type of idiot in a white coat, but as it turns out, I can read. As chair did you know the bylaws of the board state to call a board meeting, it must be presented in writing one week prior to each individual board member and announced in the newspaper to the community at least one week before the meeting?"

"Nonsense." Luft eyed Sara, who scribbled industriously in her notepad.

Beth jumped on the bandwagon. "Don't you have a parliamentarian?"

"There's no need for that, I know our bylaws."

"Apparently not." Alex appeared well pleased

with himself. "You can't have this meeting. You can discuss problems if you like, but no votes can take place."

The board members began to argue the point. Beth was mildly surprised to find Luft didn't have the following she first thought.

Alex's friend began to fire questions at Mr. Luft. Questions that were more than yes and no answers, yet she gave him only time to answer briefly. She didn't hesitate to take a few pictures, either.

Beth walked across the room to Alex as the meeting deteriorated into an argument between board members and Luft along with the newswoman.

"You've been a bad boy." She grinned at the scene before them.

With a sidelong glance, he told her, "You ain't seen nothin' yet."

Tonight's fiasco left Beth exhilarated. Never had she seen a man like Luft just give up and walk away. With his departure, the board all stopped their arguments, some in mid-sentence.

Their looks were all the same. What do we do now?

Beth announced, "I'd be glad to take any questions you may have, since this meeting to have me removed from my post will be called again. Just tell me what you want to know."

Alex, who'd just said good-bye to the newswoman, joined Beth at the head of the table. "I'm here, as well, if you need to know anything regarding the clinic, or even the pet therapy. Because the same rules apply to the last called meeting. You haven't officially voted on anything."

The members of the board first looked at each other, then back to Beth and Alex. Most of them sat down. Out of the eighteen, three left.

Good odds. Beth's thoughts whirled as she and Alex reviewed the details Luft had steamrolled over when he forced the vote on the clinic and found many of the board members receptive to a review of finances and another vote.

Almost two hours flew by as the board members took in the truth about what the community was getting from both programs. They also had the chance to see Beth in action. She explained that her figures were being used to obtain funding and grants. Her thoughts hadn't really turned to closing the clinic, or the pet therapy program.

What shocked Beth was when Alex took center stage and told the board they could elect a new chair. He explained, in explicit detail, all the bylaws regarding officers. Without actually saying the horrible things she knew he thought, Alex led the board to a conclusion that Mr. Luft was not acting in the best interests of the hospital, or the community. He finished with a presentation of a letter to the reporter detailing the clinic's problems with Mr. Luft.

She really wished he hadn't done that.

As she walked into the hospital the next morning, her cell phone rang.

"What are you wearing?" She knew the voice. It was Alex.

"Excuse me?"

"There will be lots of media at the hospital today. Here's your only warning."

"Aren't you taking this a little far into left field?"

"Are you kidding? I have no intentions of staying in the ball park." The phone clicked.

When she went to her office she found the reception area filled with a news crew, complete with cameras.

And there was Alex, grinning from ear to ear.

She sidled over to his side and murmured through a false smile toward the reporters. "Good grief, Alex, what have you gotten me into?"

"I found out an old friend of mine works at Channel Nine. She's here to do an interview. But, it's not an exclusive. There will be others as well."

Against the left wall of her office there were four chairs set up. The cameras focused there. A trim blond woman, in her mid-thirties and quite attractive, pinned a small microphone on Beth's jacket. At the same time, a guy outfitted Alex with the same.

Beth put her briefcase on the desk. "Are you sure

you want to take these chances, Alex?" She kept her voice low, fearing the mic's power.

"I'm saving my clinic at all costs."

"I can get on that soapbox with you. But, I want you to answer this, is this for Trentville? Or, is this your ego?"

The hurt was in his voice. "How can you ask me that?"

"Because more and more you call it yours. If it belongs to you, that's fine. Take it into private practice. But, if you truly have given it to the community, then any doctor can run it. With or without you."

"My dream is that clinic. To offer all I can without worrying about who pays what."

She touched his face and smiled into those blue eyes. "That's what I wanted to know. I had to be sure this hadn't come down to you versus Luft."

"It's not, Beth. It's the clinic that matters. If it meant Trentville got medical care and I went somewhere else, I would. But, this is my dream practice. I can't go it alone."

"I know you need the financial backing. I have to ask though if all of this is worth it?" She waved a hand at the news cameras.

"I have to go down fighting, Beth. It's the way I'm made."

There were things Beth could have told him.

Things that might make this battle seem superfluous, but she wouldn't take this fight from him. It had become personal and she understood his feelings.

A man who had on earphones and carried a clipboard asked Alex, "Are you ready, Dr. Price?"

He smiled at Beth, then turned to the man. "Ready as I'll ever be."

He sat across from the reporter, Beth on his other side.

"Just relax, Dr. Price."

"I'm fine," he told her. "I just want to save the clinic."

As he uttered the words, Gordon Luft entered the office. His voice blustered through the room. "What's going on in here?"

Upon seeing the cameras a look of panic crossed his face.

The reporter appeared excited. "Are you Gordon Luft?"

"I am. What's this all about?"

"My name is Cynthia Guy and we hoped you'd join us." She waved to one of the empty chairs next to Alex.

"Join you for what?" He sat down as he spoke.

"We've heard a report you will be closing the urgent care clinic, is this true?"

"Ms. Chambers is our new administrator. She has put together facts and figures to show the clinic isn't accomplishing anything for the community."

"That's not true, Cynthia." Alex didn't hesitate to defend Beth or the clinic. "As you know, the clinic cared for over a thousand people last year who are uninsured." The camera hummed as he answered her questions.

"We were called today and told that the closure of the urgent care clinic, on which the community here relies, would be voted on at the next board meeting."

"That's correct." Luft appeared happy with himself. "We're also going to vote on accepting the resignation of Miss Chambers. We already have a candidate who can fill the vacancy. One who will work with the board."

"So, you've given your notice?" The reporter turned her gaze on Beth. Out of the corner of her eye, she saw the surprise on Alex's face.

"Yes, effective in one month. I came to realize that there were purposes for my being here. One was to show the community a woman could not do this job. Two was to close the clinic and three was to dismantle the pet therapy department."

"Who offered you the job, Miss Chambers?"

"It's Beth. Mr. Luft offered me the job."

"Mr. Luft, could you elaborate?"

"I will be glad to. Miss Chambers came to us begging for a position. Being a woman in a man's world, she found herself out of work, after being *involved* with someone on her last job."

Alex flinched.

Beth saw it.

So did the newswoman. "Does this surprise you, Dr. Price?"

He bounced back. "Not really. As much as people like us are at work, who else does one meet?" He laughed.

"Miss Chambers?"

"I left my last position on very good terms. I was offered a package to stay. I'm sure they'll confirm that."

"She's a woman. She can't handle the job. She has to quit. When a woman takes administrative jobs all they're looking for is a husband. I think that Dr. Price can vouch for that."

Alex's face became solemn. "Actually, I'm not engaged to Ms. Chambers, so I can't *vouch* for anything."

"Beth, why do you feel the clinic should be closed?"

"I don't."

Luft still tried to hang Beth on this. "You were the one who had the figures. You are the one who showed me that closing the clinic would be best."

"This community needs this clinic, Cynthia. I *never* in any way led Mr. Luft to believe otherwise."

"She can't open her mouth without lying." Anger laced Gordon's words.

Cynthia spoke before anyone else could. "We

need to wrap up, so could I get some final words from each of you. Just a minute a piece, please."

Gordon spoke first. "The clinic drains this hospital of resources that could be used for paying patients."

Beth simply stated, "The clinic has a place in this community."

Alex was last. "I hope this community will come together and save their clinic. For some, it's the only medical care they can get."

"Thank you all." She paused and eyed her cameraman. "How was that, Jerry?"

He removed the headset. "It's a wrap. Very good stuff, Cynthia."

Beth took control of the men at that point. "Gordon, I've called a board meeting for you, in the appropriate manner. When you convene the meeting, you'll close the pet therapy alone."

"Are you trying to tell me what to do?"

"I think you heard me. You will cut funding to the clinic by half for the next five years and incorporate the pet therapy in the clinic's business. Then it will become freestanding. As for me, my notice is on your desk. You will have your cake and eat it too, but you will shut up and leave both Dr. Price and Dr. Thompson alone."

"What are you saying?"

"I'm giving you the proposal that Dr. Price and I had been working toward. I'm also saying you are on thin ice with the rest of the board, and all the politicking in the world may not get you back on even ground. I've found funding for the clinic and the pet therapy if they are together. Don't worry, Alex, you'll be safe." She grabbed her briefcase and left for home. She had things to do, and now that everything was set in motion, she could relax as she did them.

It sounded like an injured moose, but it was only Rhoda blowing her nose. "I can't believe you're leaving. You've been here for five years. Right next door. We've done holidays together. We've told each other everything."

"I know." Beth flopped down on her couch, next to a basket full of items to be moved. "But, Rhoda, I have to leave here. I have to know that I'm no where near Alex Price."

"You've dated before. You just went out with the guy at Christmas. It wasn't like you'd devoted your life to him."

"I love him, Rhoda. I love the way he treats his family. I love the idea of being in that family. And, I love his devotion to service. He's one of the few people I've ever met who really does things for the right reasons."

"Does he know all this?" Rhoda continued dabbing at her eyes.

"No. He knows I'm leaving the hospital. He

knows that the pet therapy will be moved to the clinic, and how it will work with all the grants both programs receive, they'll be able to keep going for the next twenty years. I explained all that last night at the board meeting. Which, by the way, was packed. They had to move it to the cafeteria. And, the rest of the board forced Luft out. He can go back to owning ten businesses in town. The Mr. Potter wannabe."

"Mr. Potter?"

"On that Jimmy Stewart movie where the angel—oh nevermind." Just talking about the movie reminded her of the wonderful evening in front of the fire with Alex.

"You're breaking my heart by leaving. I can't see you tomorrow when you leave. It'll be too hard."

"That's okay. I understand."

She stood and the two women embraced for several minutes. Rhoda felt like the only family she'd had since her aunt's death, she didn't want to leave. Not like this.

But, her logical side knew that this would be for the best. When she'd left her last position, she'd been disconcerted, not broken-hearted.

Now she found, there was truly a difference.

As Rhoda opened the door to leave Beth's apartment, she had to duck to avoid Alex's hand, raised to knock.

After a moment of surprise they both recouped.

Alex had a buddy with him. Joey the pig immediately passed by Rhoda and laid down on Beth's feet.

Rhoda glanced up at him and patted his arm. "I'm glad you're here." She looked at Beth over her shoulder, but other than a raised eyebrow said nothing before she left.

"Joey knew I wouldn't be seeing you anymore, so he asked me to bring him by." He took a good look around him at the boxes and bags all over the room.

"Are you moving?"

"Yes." She sat down on the couch and Joey jumped up beside her. He rested his head on her lap as she stroked his snout.

"You weren't going to tell me, were you?" Alex remained standing.

"There's nothing to tell. I've taken a job in Louisville as Assistant Administrator at Louisville General. A dream job to be sure. If you can find a place, have a seat."

He sat in the chair Rhoda vacated. "I can't believe you would've left without saying good-bye."

"No reason to drag this out, Alex. I'm leaving in the morning. It's not like we ever made it past the first date."

"I'm in love with you."

"Alex, you're really making this hard. I can't base my career on your feelings."

"Or yours?" He looked down into her eyes.

She looked away. "Or mine."

An uncomfortable silence fell on the room. Finally he stood. "Well, I guess I'll just say bye and hope . . . and wish you well."

Her heart broke. Couldn't he beg her to stay?

"I wish you all the best and the clinic as well. Thanks again, for Christmas."

"My pleasure." His voice held no hint of his feelings.

He left. He walked out the door. He closed the door. And, he was gone.

So, now what did she do? Joey grunted. "What—?"

Joey refused to move as she tried to get up to catch Alex. Finally, she pushed him gently aside, ran for the door and opened it. Alex stood on the other side.

"You forgot your pig!"

"I didn't forget him, it was the only way I knew to get you to come after me." He took her in his arms. "Don't leave me and you'll never be sorry."

Joey squealed and plopped down next to their feet.

"But, I have a job waiting on me."

"Think of this—here you have me, the clinic, Joey, and my entire family who will love you. No job can give you that, Beth. Nothing can replace what you need. It's not things. It's me."

"You think I *need* you?" She snuggled into his arms, totally negating any resistance she was supposed to be giving.

"I'm betting my entire emotional well-being on it." He tightened his hold.

"And, what will I do with my life while you play doctor?"

"You'll work out of the clinic. You'll consult, write grants, and love me."

Joey snorted.

He amended, "And, Joey, of course."

"You seem to have this all planned out."

His tone playful, he told her, "Hey, I wouldn't approach a woman of your position without one. It's how you thrive."

"You aren't even sure you love me."

"When you told me you were leaving, I realized that I couldn't go on without you."

He kissed her. Wrapped tightly in his arms, she realized there was no other place she wanted to be.

"Marry me, Beth, you'll never be sorry."

"Then I'll never be sorry."

Clothes, cars, jobs, they were all necessary to life, but not life itself. Love, family, even a little pig, that's what made living worthwhile.

Tears fell on her cheeks as she realized what the path she chose would bring.

He held her face in his hands, wiping her tears away with his thumbs. "You okay?"

"I've never felt like this before. You're the doctor," she joked, "What do you think it is?"

"Definitely the bad stuff. The diagnosis is love."

As his lips met hers again, Beth knew he was right.